ICE CREAM FOR REFUGEES

Daniele J. Grassi was born in 1987 in Austria but grew up in Italy where he attended an international school and discovered a passion for writing through a witty South Carolinian literature teacher. After almost a decade spent studying and working abroad, he moved back to his native Austria and accepted a position as a government official. Before writing Ice Cream for Refugees, Daniele was the chief of staff of the Austrian government spokesperson.

DANIELE J. GRASSI

ICE CREAM FOR REFUGEES

A NOVEL

The future belongs to those who believe in the beauty of their dreams.

-Eleanor Roosevelt

To Roberto Grassi

ONE

On top of an artificial hill in the center of the rural village of Maisland stood a futuristic building made predominantly of concrete, glass, and carbon fiber. It was by far the most cutting-edge construction within a hundred-mile radius, while at the same time a punch in the eye to anybody with even a minute sense of aesthetics. The Maisland Bulletin, a biweekly local newspaper with a modest circulation of nine hundred and fifty copies, had called it 'a surprisingly ugly building with the charms of a second world war bunker'. In contrast, all the houses in the proximity of the visionary town hall had fallen prey to the irreversible deeds of time, including Madame Theresa's ice cream parlor and Wolfgang's hunting and fishing gear shop.

Maisland was not exactly one of those idyllic mountain villages that come to mind from postcards or *Heidi and*

Peter reruns. It was nestled at the lowest point of a remote valley in the middle of Austria, which coincidentally was also in the middle of nowhere. Most Maislanders were farmers who prided themselves on the fact that they would survive the upcoming collapse of the financial system due to their ability to grow vegetables and raise cattle. Recently, they had also started to pride themselves on their new town hall. They didn't understand the architecture and evidently didn't know how much it cost, but it was new, shiny, and unequivocally theirs.

The top floor of the lavish building was occupied by the office of Mayor Franz Bauer, whom over the past four years had occasionally reigned with a childish nonchalance over the three thousand inhabitants of Maisland. Due to a lack of funds to hire new employees, the remaining rooms on the first two floors of the bold town hall were mostly uninhabited and used by friends of the mayor to store hay from the previous seasons and grain to feed their cattle.

Franz Bauer was a beloved son of the tiny mountain village.

Slightly overweight with thick, reddish curly hair, he was the type of man fellow Maislanders respected: smart enough to make promises he couldn't keep but also not smart enough to enrich himself in the process.

Building a new town hall was one of the first items on his agenda when he took office, and most Maislanders fell in love with the young man's energy and passion. Before returning to his native village to take over his father's ranch and run for office, he had spent nine years in the provincial capital of Graz, studying agricultural business and socializing his way into the People's Freedom Party. The countless nights he had spent drinking beer and shots of stone pine schnapps with his comrades secured him a strong political backing that eventually gave him the confidence to make his way back from the two-hour away Graz without a degree but armed with great determination.

Franz Bauer was no longer the shy boy who spent most of his teenage years petting baby goats and hiding out in his treehouse. He'd had a glance of the big wide world and was back with fresh ideas for Maisland and its proud inhabitants.

Although the day had started off like any other - with a glass of fresh milk and a slice of dark bread with a thick layer of butter - on this particular day, Franz had a funny feeling in his gut. As he whipped the mustache of milk from his lip, a lifeless voice made its way into his office. "Good morning Franz."

"Hello to you Jenny, you look especially lovely today!" he replied while scanning his young secretary from head to toe.

Jenny was the daughter of Madame Theresa, and although she had inherited the old lady's blue eyes and blond hair, she had the figure of an inverted ice cream cone. Last year, after she graduated from Alfons Haider high school, her mother tried to force her to leave Maisland for Vienna, so she could experience something new, but she firmly refused. She was comfortable in the village, where she enjoyed a steady and cheap supply of weed and ice cream. Since that wasn't really a strong argument to put to her mother, she pretended to be pregnant as long as it was physically possible. But nine months passed, and on the day she was supposed to give birth, she finally told her mother the truth. By then, it was too late for her to leave; she had already accepted a prestigious position at the town hall.

"Your award for most diverse sheep cattle has arrived. Where should I put it?" she asked.

Franz looked at the framed document with a mix of excitement and satisfaction. Finally, all the effort he had put in these past years to form a homogenous mix of heritage and fur color had paid off.

"Maybe next to the certificate for the most unique town hall of the valley."

"The one from last year or the year before?" she asked without expression.

Franz snorted, annoyed. He hated the mayor of the neighboring town of Goldau, Arnold Kraut. His win in this year's edition was no surprise. Kraut had built his new town hall in the form of a horseshoe, and the jury loved it. 'What a bunch of farmers,' he thought.

"From two years ago," he shouted.

To reach the wall, Jenny had to walk around a labyrinth of boxes and tiny statues.

"The room is getting really full of awards and framed interviews Franz. Maybe you should get rid of some of the less impressive ones, like the interview with *Bratwurst & Shotguns*?"

"Are you an interior designer? I didn't hire you for that!" he barked.

"No, you hired me because there was nobody else that wanted to work for you," she replied.

Franz didn't have the best reputation as an employer. Before convincing Jenny to take the position as his secretary as well as manager of Maisland's social media pages, he was infamous for going through fourteen secretaries in less than four years. To his credit, some of them left because they got pregnant or decided to leave Maisland, but most of them just hated that he was so melodramatic.

"That will be all, thank you!"

"Oh yes, one more thing," she said. "The Commodore called earlier today. He needs to talk to you urgently."

Franz lit up.

The man that went by the nickname 'the Commodore' was the regional head of the People's Freedom Party. Franz had met him during his second year in Graz and worshiped him for his intelligence and style. When he eventually returned home to run for office, the Commodore secured him backing from the party and made it ultimately possible for him to sit in that overpaid position, surrounded by all those useless awards.

He picked up the phone and dialed his number.

"Franzi my Franzi…" the Commodore crooned.

"How are you?" Franz asked hesitantly.

"I am very well, thank you. I must tell you, my birthday party over the weekend was really something."

Franz felt tightness in his throat. He had completely forgotten about the Commodore's birthday.

"I hope you like the card I sent you?" he lied after being quiet for what was clearly an awkward amount of time.

"What card? I didn't receive anything from you, my Franzi."

"There must have been some sort of mistake, let me check with…"

"No worries, everything is fine. No big deal," the Commodore interrupted him. "But I was thinking, my dear Franzi, you are facing elections soon…"

Franz breathed a sigh of relief. From his experience, the Commodore was not the type of man who took disrespect lightly. He had once witnessed him firing an employee because he had mispronounced the name of his beloved Labrador Aishwarya.

"I am indeed. It will be a hole-in-one, again," Franz said.

The young mayor couldn't believe his luck. The Commodore had lashed out on him several times for things far less important than forgetting his birthday.

"Well, I was thinking. You know how the party is positioning itself a bit more to the left lately?" the Commodore asked.

"It is?"

Although the young mayor was no expert on politics, the sole action of mentioning his political party and the word left in the same sentence caused alarm bells. The Maisland Bulletin had once written that the People's Freedom Party was so right on the left-right political spectrum that it might be already left again.

"Well yes, we realized that all this talk about being open to immigration and integrating migrants is resonating with the voters."

A silence fell between the two men.

"It would be great if you would jump on this train with us, my Franzi," he continued.

"Of course, of course. You know I'll do anything for you, Commodore. What do you need me to do?"

"I'm happy to hear that. We were thinking of building a welcome center for refugees in Maisland."

As soon as that last word came out through the receiver, every fiber of every muscle in Franz Bauer's body froze. He felt like a deer, blinded by the headlights of the car that is about to run him down. He tried to catch his breath, but his heart was beating too quickly. He had a million questions, but nothing would come out of his mouth.

"What do you mean refugees? How many? And from where?" he finally said with a weak voice.

"Well, it's hard to say. A couple of hundred, perhaps. And I think most of them are from Afghanistan and Syria."

What the… Franz was screaming in his head.

"Thanks for the offer, Commodore. Although I wasn't aware of it, I'm sure that it is a positive move towards the new orientation of the party. Nonetheless, I am essentially running unopposed, so there is really no need for gestures like this. Maybe this would be something for Arnold Kraut. I hear he has quite the competition when it comes…"

"But Franzi, it has been decided already. This comes directly from Vienna, there's no point discussing it!"

Rage overtook Franzi. The knuckles on his fist had turned white from clenching so hard, and his face was the color of an over-ripe tomato.

"Are you kidding me? Because I forgot your birthday?"

"This has nothing to do with my birthday, how dare you?" the Commodore said.

"So, what the hell is this crap? Are you kidding me?"

The Commodore took his time before calmly replying.

"The center must be ready in six months. If I hear one more word from you, I will make you build a mosque as well!"

Franz disconnected and slid into his chair feeling utterly desperate.

"Jenny!" he screamed.

"What is it?" she squealed back, clearly annoyed.

"Set up an emergency town hall meeting for tomorrow night!"

TWO

When Franz arrived at the village's *Festhalle* there was a buzz of excitement in the air. Trucks, bicycles, and tractors were parked almost on top of each other, and every man and woman seemed to have an open can of beer in their left hand and a cigarette in their right.

The last time he had called a town hall assembly, he had announced his intention to break the Guinness World Record for the longest *Strudel,* and the crowd exploded in exhilaration. Events like that resonated widely with Maislanders because they attracted visitors and media to their remote village and gave them a well-deserved chance to drink rivers of alcohol for no significant reason.

Anything out the ordinary that would happen in Maisland took place in the *Festhalle*. Folk music concerts, carnival parties, and eating contests were among the most popular events. The building was timbered and in terrible condition, sprawled around an uneven and, due to its inclination, relatively dangerous parking lot. Most of the wood encasing the outside walls and roof had rotted decades ago, and a thick layer of green mold covered the structure like a fuzzy blanket. Franz would obviously never admit it to anybody, but every Sunday, in church, he would light a candle praying that the roof doesn't suddenly fall onto people during one of the many events - at least not as long as he was mayor.

On that particular night, the *Festhalle* was unbelievably crowded. The last time Franz had seen so many people in there was for the David Hasselhoff concert two years before, where he was among the two thousand people singing the Baywatch theme song at the top of their lungs. The noise was so powerful that the walls trembled as if shook by an earthquake.

As he was about to address over a thousand people that stood waiting, stuffed like pickles in a jar, someone grabbed his arm, and he turned to see a familiar face.

"People are talking Franz," Madame Theresa whispered in his ear. "Do you want to know what they are saying?"

The owner of Maisland's ice cream parlor was a colorful character and, without a doubt, a pillar of the community. Although she was only in her forties, her skin was already creased and leathery. She insisted that it had to do with the low temperatures she was exposed to every day at the parlor, but the two packs of Marlboros she smoked, day in and day out, and the frequent visits to the tanning salon surely contributed.

He peered at her sneaky face, not unlike a weasel. "Tell me, what are they saying."

She clutched his arm like an insecure lover and paused dramatically. As he waited, he noticed that her makeup was every shade of wrong imaginable. Who wears blue eye shadow anymore? He imagined her dancing in an 80s music video: big hair, bright lips.

In Franz's eyes, she was the one person that knew everything about everybody - not because people turned to her with their deepest secrets, but because she had an unnatural ferocity in finding out the latest gossip. Some villagers had even speculated that she actually hated ice cream and only opened her parlor to be able to listen in on people's conversations.

"Are you building a new community center for the village?" she asked, giving him a flirty wink.

"What?"

"I also heard that it will be a new *Festhalle*? Is it true?"

Franz looked around nervously. He should have made it clear from the beginning that this was not going to be a pleasant social town-hall meeting. The Commodore had always taught him that managing expectations was one of the most important prerequisites of a good politician.

"You know we don't have money for that," he replied.

"But this one is in such terrible shape. I can't believe it's still standing. If you ask me, it is just a matter of time until it collapses."

The mayor looked upwards. Most of the wooden boards on the ceiling had turned gray and exposed massive cracks. His heart sank.

"Well, I didn't." Franz replied.

"You didn't what?"

"Ask you."

"Come on Franz, don't be so grumpy. The reason I am asking is because I heard something very suspicious."

"Spit it out, I don't have a lot of time. I need to get on stage."

Madame Theresa grabbed his arm and slowly rubbed her thumb on the inside of his wrist in an awkward attempt to create a sensual connection between them. At the same time, she moved her lips even closer to Franz's ear, which made him extraordinarily uncomfortable. Not to mention her breath smelled sour and smoky, causing his throat to close.

"Apparently, somebody from Vienna offered a lot of money to Wolfgang for his building plot next to the sports center," she whispered.

Franz twisted his mouth. "Shit!"

"What? You didn't know?"

The young mayor tried to move along towards the podium, but Madame Theresa wouldn't let go of his arm.

"Wait honey! If you are not building something on that huge plot, then who is?"

He tugged his arm free and left her standing there to ponder.

As Franz walked up on the tiny stage Jenny had set up for him earlier that day, the crowd got louder and started clapping.

"Please everybody, calm down," Franz said into the microphone.

The noise only got stronger.

"Franz Bauer – our man of the hour!" the crowd was now chanting.

Franz was slowly getting anxious. His mind blurred as the crowd became the buzz of thousands of bees. He pressed his palms against his temples and shook his head to regain composure.

"OK that's enough, everyone, thanks!"

Over the past four years, the young mayor had desperately tried to keep Maislanders happy. Although he hadn't made any significant improvements in terms of infrastructure, safety, education, and healthcare, he managed to exponentially increase the entertainment factor. Among the many events that were brought to life since he took office, the most successful one was the *Knödel* eating contest. Contrary to traditional eating contests, Franz's edition did not include a strict time limit. To win the contest, which the Maisland Bulletin had kindly dubbed 'the marathon of eating', competitors were given twenty-four hours to eat as many boiled dumplings as they can. Contestants are also allowed and grotesquely encouraged to relieve themselves from any opening of the body – as long as they do it on stage. Needless to say, that it was the crudeness and bestiality of the event that compelled thousands of visitors to attend each year. By the end of the event, the makeshift stage was a train wreck.

"I heard that a lot of you think that I will be building a new *Festhalle*," he continued.

The villagers unanimously rose to their feet in a standing ovation. Franz paused and gazed into the distance. His heart was pounding like a jackhammer. In the second to last row, two young Maislanders held up colorful signs that read: 'Franz Bauer, Our Man'.

The mayor blushed. His shoulders slumped as he moved his head closer to the microphone. "Well, that's not happening. There is something else that I have to communicate to you."

Franz paused again and looked down to the front row. Among the many familiar faces, he spotted a surprisingly pleased Wolfgang. Although he was very fond of the hunting and fishing gear shop owner, there was something about his enigmatic grin that alarmed Franz. He tried to stare him straight in the eye, contorting his lips into what felt like an awkward, toothy smile, but Wolfgang promptly looked away, leaving Franz feeling as neglected as a Jehovah's Witness on the doorstep.

"We will be building something, but it won't be a new *Festhalle*," he continued with an over decisive tone.

"Will it be a bowling alley?" a young man shouted euphorically.

The whole room burst into cheers again, and Franz's abdominal muscles contracted.

"No, people. It won't be anything for entertainment."

A woman in the second row stood up from her chair. "Are we getting a new community center? Arnold Kraut just built an amazing new facility in Goldau!"

The young mayor closed his eyes to block out the ridiculous demands.

The woman didn't seem to be concerned about his deteriorating body language and continued. "It has indoor and outdoor pools, a computer room, saunas, an open-air cinema, a climbing wall, a go-kart track, and a wave pool for surfing. I think that we should consider…"

"We're building a welcome center for refugees," Franz said into the microphone.

The room went dead silent.

THREE

The baby goat had green eyes. A very unusual shade of green, Franz thought. It was not like a pine-tree green or fresh moss. It was more like a glazed-lime or a Granny-Smith-apple, a vivid reminder of beautiful landscapes and of the freshness and vitality of life itself.

The young mayor looked around. Clouds. As far as his eyes could see. The only thing around him that was not made of cold vapor was a red carpet under his feet. In the middle of the grandiose tapestry, which seemed to be stretching itself out to infinity, stood a baby goat.

Herded by a strong sense of curiosity and excitement, Franz sprinted towards the mesmerizing creature. Amid the exhilaration, a strong pain shot from the back of his head.

"Don't worry about it, you are fine!" bleated the tiny goat. The animal was soft-spoken and had the aura of an angelical being.

Franz resisted the overpowering urge to touch the magical creature.

"Why do you speak so nicely?" he asked.

"Because I want you to understand what I am about to say," the goat replied. The beautiful melody of the bleat had an anesthetizing effect on Franz. He completely forgot about the pain in his head.

He kneeled. "What is it that you want to tell me, little goat?" he spoke back in the same soft tone.

"Please don't call me goat. Call me Babsi."

Franz blushed.

"I'm sorry, Babsi. You are so angelic." He paused. "What is it that you want to tell me?"

The goat reared up and peered at Franz.

The mayor narrowed his eyes too, in confusion. Was he really seeing what he thought he was seeing?

"Can I touch you?" he asked.

The tiny goat calmly shook its head.

"Those refugees will destroy your beautiful Maisland if you don't do something about it," Babsi announced firmly.

Franz was in a trance. The headache had disappeared, but a feeling of loneliness and rejection swept through his body.

"So, what am I supposed to do? Please help me," he said feebly.

The creature nodded its head in approval.

"You have to encourage them to become Maislanders," the goat bleated with a magical echo and disappeared.

Franz woke up with a monumental headache to the sound of the church bells, and it took him a couple of seconds to realize he was lying on his office floor.

He touched his head: blood. He must have slipped last night while running into the town hall after the disaster at the *Festhalle*. Just thinking about the night before doubled the intensity of his headache.

After his big announcement, the people had fallen silent. He was just about to explain the new direction of the People's Freedom Party and the long-term benefits for Maisland, but before he could open his mouth, a cucumber cracked the side of his face. The bloody nerve! And then chaos prevailed. Everybody was shouting and pounding amidst the flying vegetables and beer cans. The pinnacle of the pandemonium, which coincidentally was also the moment Franz stormed to the exit, was reached when a group of elders fired their hunting rifles into the ceiling – not to calm down the crowd but as a protest.

"Jenny!" he now shouted

The young secretary was only a couple of meters away, sitting comfortably on a lounge chair while reading her favorite gossip magazine.

"Oh, you're awake. Good morning," she said with a toneless voice and without moving her gaze from the magazine.

Franz looked at her in disbelief. "I am bleeding! Did you think I was taking a nap?"

"Sorry. I thought you were too drunk to drive and slept here – just like after the corn festival, or the ski jumping world cup or…"

"It's ok Jenny, I'm fine. Thank you." The mayor got up from the floor, brushed off his shirt, and started walking around the room. The vision he had just experienced was still extremely vivid and clear in his mind.

"I think I know what we have to do," he said in a triumphant tone.

"About what?" Jenny asked.

"About the refugees, what else?"

"Oh yeah, right. So, what's your brilliant idea?"

Franz rubbed his hands together. "If we can't fight this whole refugee thing, then let's try and make the best of it."

Jenny turned and stared him down with a confused and yet still lifeless look.

"Let's educate them. Teach them about our traditions and culture, so it is easier for them to adapt. We have to help them to become Maislanders!" he continued.

"And how should we do that?"

"I don't know, maybe you have a good idea? You're young and have a fresh view of the world."

Jenny closed her magazine and struck a thinking pose. "Maybe we could give them something like a manual? And then some coaching."

Franz could barely conceal his delight. "A manual is a great idea, well done!" he whooped.

Jenny was clearly not impressed with her genius.

"And who is going to write it?" she asked.

The mayor caressed his beard. "I think we need to get some experts to write it for us. Maybe after that, they could also hold some lessons for them. I don't see any other way of doing it."

"We don't have any money for that," Jenny replied, determined to kill his buzz.

"What do you mean there is no money, how much do we have left?"

"Maybe around five thousand."

Franz's stomach twisted. "What? And where is the rest of the budget?"

"The World Record..." she replied.

Franz shook his head in self-disappointment. He had forgotten about the *Strudel*. Looking back, it probably wasn't the best idea to spend a mountain of money to sponsor a Guinness World Record for an exceptionally long pastry. He ended up having to buy an industrial oven the size of a truck, about half a ton of apples, a quarter of a ton of cream cheese, and hiring forty-five cooks.

"I understand. Do you know anybody who understands their culture? And could write it for a reasonable price? Let's just forget about the coaching part."

"What do you mean somebody that understands their culture?"

"You know what I mean, somebody from …"

"Like a black person?" Jenny said.

Franz shrugged. "No, not necessarily black…I mean, yes black but not like African black," he replied.

"Ah, I understand what you mean."

Jenny re-struck a thinking pose.

"You do?"

"Yeah! I've seen a brown guy a couple of times at Pizza Hawaii. Should I ask him?" she continued.

"Wonderful! Could you please bring him in as soon as possible?" Franz was thrilled.

"Sure! By the way I have a letter for you from my mother."

"Her ice cream parlor is literally one minute away, why doesn't she just come over?" he asked.

"Well because she is my mother, I don't want her to come to my workplace – that's not cool. Get it?"

Jenny gave him the letter and waltzed off.

Dear Franz,

The reason I am writing you this letter and not coming over to your office is that I am extremely busy. You know, early spring is a hell of a time for ice cream parlors. I hope you don't think that I'm not coming because Jenny doesn't want me to. That would be ridiculous! It's really not her fault. She is a good girl.

As you can imagine, I am writing you because of last night. It was quite the show at the Festhalle. Shortly after you left, one of the elders fired his rifle again and hit the big chandelier. Fortunately, it only fell on Martin's right leg - which had to be amputated - but everyone else was unharmed. By the way, I think Martin is going to sue you or the city, or probably both. Thank god that new young officer of the police department, Günther Frank, was there. He managed to calm everybody down a little.

Anyway, since you left early, which I really didn't understand because there were a lot of people that wanted to talk to you, I guess I have to ask my questions this way.
How many refugees are coming? Do they like ice cream?
Will they use our church, or will they build a new one? I wouldn't mind having a new church, to be completely

honest. Maybe we could also exchange Father Benedikt. He has the charisma of a dead raccoon and always tries to sell me his holy water.

If they happen to not like ice cream, can we somehow make it mandatory for them to eat it?

Also, I heard that some of them are violent towards women. Do you think that it will be risky for us women to walk around Maisland? I mean I dated guys that got a little aggressive after drinking and I've been shaken up a couple of times before, but they were my boyfriends! Getting knocked around by a complete stranger is not the same thing. I don't think I would be OK with that.

I am looking forward to your answers.

In the meantime, if you feel like ice cream or anything else, you know where to find me ;)

Hugs and Kisses,
Theresa

FOUR

Wolfgang's resistance movement, More Guns, Less Refugees, took off unexpectedly and with a bang. What had started off as a drunken conversation at Jörg's Pub the night after the *Festhalle* disaster had turned into a political avalanche, which was about to hit Maisland at the speed of light.

In a mix of alcohol-induced courage, the relatively shy hunting and fishing gear shop owner had taken hold of the karaoke microphone and delivered a rather flowery and declamatory speech. Standing on top of the bar and deploying keywords like Austria, homeland, forefathers, and culture, he was able to pull off quite the show and secure himself the attention of the guests and even earn a couple of energetic handclaps. He had no idea what had come over him. Perhaps it was just a weariness for life that he had been feeling recently, or a curious desire to see what it felt like to be adamant about something, to be black and white in his thinking instead of entertaining every possibility. Afterward, he wondered if he just wanted to be someone else for a while. He had finished up his monologue by inviting the whole pub to the first meeting of the resistance movement, and now, not even 24 hours later, around a hundred people had stormed into the basement of his shop.

"I didn't expect so many of you to come," he said, a little embarrassed while pointing at the buffet. The folding table, covered with a green sniper concealment blanket, displayed ten paper cups in one corner, a half-full box of cookies on the other, and a fairly large sausage and a hunting knife in the middle.

"Feel free to serve yourself, my comrades!"

The unlikely knight in shining armor was standing tall on a large wooden ammunition box, in full hunting attire. Under the shadow of his jungle hat, he was showing off a pair of Oakley sunglasses with sunset yellow lenses. Although he was perfectly geared up for a bear hunting expedition, to an unbiased observer, something wouldn't have seemed right. His fragile body structure, perfectly trimmed, brown mustache, and big kind eyes made him look more like an honest and trustworthy university professor than a heartless hunter.

"Many thanks to you all for coming. I have the feeling that this is the start of a thrilling and provocative journey," he said while looking around the room to do a quick headcount.

His newly gained followers started clapping and high fiving each other. The energy in the room was palpable. The levels of testosterone were off the charts, and Wolfgang felt the chills wandering down his spine, boosting his confidence to a new high.

"Who in here is happy not to follow the mainstream agenda, and to not facilitate the integration of people with a migration background, but to support the development of a constructive and long-term nationally oriented narrative?" he shouted.

Silence.

It seemed like there was great confusion in the room. Some people raised their hand just a little while desperately looking around for confirmation, and Wolfgang promptly decided to give it another try, this time using a more direct approach in combination with a simpler word choice.

"Who in here doesn't want refugees?" he screamed.

The cheering was overwhelming. Hands were almost reaching the ceiling, and Wolfgang didn't think twice about riding the wave of excitement.

"We don't need and don't want refugees here. Maisland is ours, and it should stay that way!" he screamed. "If they think that we will let a couple of hundred refugees come here and attack the way we live, they are wrong!" he continued.

The crowd nodded energetically.

In Wolfgang's mind, it was now time to address the real issue with the refugee center and to initiate a constructive dialogue in Maisland.

"You all know me, I'm not a violent guy," he started off. "I just happen to own a hunting gear shop." His voice became soft and compassionate. "The reason I invited all of you to the basement of my shop is because I want us to make use of our right to peacefully protest and to challenge the democratic component of the decision to build the welcome center."

Silence again.

In the middle of the crowd, a young woodworker Wolfgang knew well raised his hand.

"Hello, my dear, good to see you. How are you, my friend? Go ahead with your question," he said.

"Hello to you!" the young man said. "Well, to be honest, not that great. I had a work accident last week and lost two fingers," he continued in a slightly less enthusiastic tone.

Murmurs of solidarity erupted in the crowd.

"That's awful, I am so sorry to hear. I hope you are recovering well."

"I am, thank you. I have been drinking a lot of Gatorade, which is supposed to help the skin regenerate."

Wolfgang gifted him a half-hearted smile. "I am not sure that is the case, but yeah, I'm sure it tastes refreshing - at least that's what I read. Anyway, what was your question?"

The young man knit his brows together. "I don't remember. It all went down so fast. But probably something like: is the machine still on?"

Wolfgang's nose and forehead scrunched up. "What?"

"The question I asked before losing my fingers."

"I meant the question you wanted to ask when you raised your hand... just now."

"Oh yeah, sorry," the young man said, his face blushing. "I wanted to know what a democratic component is?"

Numerous heads around the young man nodded. Wolfgang froze.

Disbelief spread across his face as he glanced into the distance.

Loving Maisland was probably the only thing he had in common with most of his co-villagers. Not that it really bothered him. He spent most of his days reading academic papers on astrophysics, so he wasn't overly keen on socializing with his acquaintances anyway.

Born into a relatively simple but respected Maislander family, the young Wolfgang never really felt like an integral part of his environment. Shortly after his ninth birthday, he had told his mother that he was looking forward to leaving Maisland at some point and move to

Austria's capital Vienna to start an information technology company - something that was so ahead of its time and of everybody else's understanding, that his mother immediately took him to see a couple of specialists, not in Vienna of course, but locals who had their own brew of expertise.

By the time he turned sixteen, he had skipped four grades and spent a couple of years at the public library reading every single book he could find in the building, slowing his planned departure from the village. The more he read, though, the more he realized that wherever he went, he would likely only find sadness and disappointment, so he ultimately decided to remain in Maisland.

One day, while taking an online language course in advanced Aramaic, he had the clear idea to open a shop for hunting and fishing gear. Although he was a pacifist to his core and hated anything related to fish, to him, his decision made absolute sense. When people close to him at the time asked him about his decision, he would simply reply that positive anything is better than negative nothing.

He was also way too smart to hate refugees. At the end of the day, they were just people, often fleeing from war zones to find a better life for themselves and their families. How could he condemn that? But as much as he felt compassion towards them, he was also bored out of his mind, and even he knew that boredom looked for trouble. Not to mention that he quite liked the attention he had been receiving since his outburst at the pub. "It doesn't matter, my friends!" he screamed. "What matters is that we will defend our houses and our families with force!" he continued.

The crowd exploded in cheer, and Wolfgang felt that excitement in his gut again. That special something he had been feeling since the night before at the pub. The feeling of being somebody others looked up to. A feeling he had never experienced before in his life.

In his mind, he was the type of smart that people detested. He had once written an academic paper about it, which he submitted incognito to Wharton's Psychology Review. His hypothesis was that exceptionally smart people could be divided into three categories, depending on how smart they were. The least smart of the geniuses were the type of smart that people respected. The average smart people among the geniuses were the type of smart that people feared and the smartest kind of geniuses, were the type of smart that people detested. Ultimately, the paper collected so much hatred and despise that it had to be awarded the prestigious 'paper of the century' award.

"But how are we going to defend ourselves, I only have an ax at home?" a middle-aged man with a large neck tattoo screamed.

Amidst the murmurs of the guests, another voice emerged from the crowd. "And I only have a grass hook!"

Wolfgang waited for his brain to instantly draw up a virtual SWOT analysis. Arming uneducated and aggressive people was definitely not a decision that should be taken lightly, so he decided to give it at least a couple of seconds of thought. Since the whole idea of the movement was not rationally driven from the start, he promptly dismissed the non-relevant elements of the SWOT analysis, namely the strengths, weaknesses and threats. What remained was an opportunity with a capital O.

"OK friends, tonight and only tonight I'll discount all rifles, guns and knives by 70%!"

The comrades started clapping so loud, that the noise made its way from the tiny cellar of the shop all the way up to Maisland's main square. It was the wee hours of the night, so most of the villagers were sleeping. The only other source of light came from a window on top of Madame Theresa's ice cream parlor where she was awake writing a letter.

Dear Franz,

I hope it is fine that I took the liberty of writing you again. I am still too busy to come by your office.

There has been a lot of suspicious activity here in Maisland in the past couple of days, and I think you should be aware of it.

As you well know, it's not really ice cream season, so I have a lot of free time, and I love to keep an eye on what's happening in our beautiful village.

Just now, while I was watching the third season of The Bold and the Beautiful in my underwear with a bottle of champagne and cashew nuts, I saw a lot of movement in front of Wolfgang's shop. People were going in and out and loading up wooden boxes in the back of their cars. Might I add that it's 2 a.m.

You know that I'm not fond of Wolfgang, and it has nothing to do with the fact that he thinks he's too smart to buy ice cream – I swear! There is really something going on there in his hunting shop. Now obviously, I have no idea what was in those boxes, that's anybody's guess, but I think you should keep him on your radar.

By the way, I wanted to let you know again how much I appreciate what you' re doing for those poor refugees by building them a welcome center.

A big and wet kiss ;)
Theresa

FIVE

Franz narrowed his eyes. He was genuinely confused by the man sitting in front of him. Certain attributes of his presence deviated from the picture he had in his mind of how a refugee should look like. The man's skin was definitely too dark for him to be a Maislander, and that was clearly the reason Jenny had brought him in in the first place. What did puzzle Franz, however, was the color of his hair and eyes. His hair was just too blond, and his eyes too blue to resemble one of those asylum seekers he saw in the news.

Franz tried to pull off his most welcoming smile.

"Hello welcome to my office, what is your name?"

"Luigi," the man replied.

The man was not particularly tall, nor was he in good shape but had a great sense of style - at least that's what Franz thought. He was sporting a blue t-shirt with an

Italian flag, way too small and tight to fully cover his big belly. But his stomach wasn't the only sizable thing the man was exhibiting. He also wore a massive gold watch and a necklace with a cross pendant covered in what Franz assumed to be real diamonds.

The mayor scratched his beard. "That's quite the interesting name, very catchy. Certainly not a name I have heard before. Why don't you tell me a little bit about yourself, would you?" he asked.

The man didn't seem particularly interested in Franz or the conversation. He was gazing off into the distance blankly.

"My name is Luigi. I have been living in Goldau for seven years, and I work at Pizza Hawaii," he replied.

Franz slouched back in his chair and sighed. He hated hearing the name Goldau. There were a lot of reasons he despised the neighboring village but above all was its new mayor, Arnold Kraut. The young Kraut was tall, handsome, smart, and an up-and-coming star within the regional People's Freedom Party. He had won last year's elections in a landslide and was not only the Commodore's new darling but also considered to be next in line to become regional chief. Thinking about Kraut gave Franz shivers. And it wasn't like he was jealous of his young, handsome counterpart. He just hated him because he was everything he always wanted to be.

"Oh Goldau, what a nice town!" he lied. "And how are they treating you, do you like your job?" he continued.

"I hate it," the man replied deadpan.

"Why is that?"

The man leaned forward, as if he were about to tell Franz the darkest secret of his life.

"They make me put pineapple on pizzas." He looked the mayor straight in the eye.

"Pineapple! Can you imagine how that feels?"

Franz loved Pizza with pineapple. It reminded him of the hot summer evenings he spent in Maisland when he was a teenager. All he would eat those days was pizza with pineapple and spaghetti ice cream.

"Yeah, I know exactly what you mean…pineapple, are they crazy?" Franz said.

The man brought the fingertips of his right hand together and waved his hand.

"Yes, that is what I say. I learned how to make pizza in Naples, and they would kill me if they knew."

Franz's eyes lit up in surprise.

"Oh wow, you traveled all the way to Naples to learn how to bake Pizza? If that is not a commitment, then I don't know what is. Good for you!"

The man gave Franz a blank look.

"What?"

"You will be happy to hear that, if you want, we could hire you as a special consultant," the mayor continued.

The man shrugged. "Special consultant for what?"

"Well, you probably heard about the refugee center we are building."

The man burst out in laughter. "Yes, of course! Last night Arnold Kraut made a funny joke about it at the pizzeria; he said that Maislanders had already started learning Arabic."

A vortex of anger swirled inside Franz.

"OK enough!" he shouted. "I'll get to the point. As a refugee that has lived here long enough, I want you to write a manual for…"

The pizza chef quickly waved off the young mayor. "Refugee? What are you talking about?" he said in a slightly irritated tone.

The mayor took a deep breath. "Let me explain," he said in a dulcet tone. "I want you to write a manual for the refugees on how to become a Maislander. To teach them about our culture and explain to them how to behave here."

The man shook his head.

"Wait, wait I think you got this wrong, my *amico*, I am not a…"

"We have a budget of five thousand," Franz snapped, interrupting the man.

As soon as the last word came out of the mayor's mouth, the pizza chef from Goldau went silent. He leaned back into his chair and looked at Franz with a disingenuous smile.

"Mr. Mayor, I think that's a great idea. I wish somebody would have given me a manual when I moved here from…I mean you know, where a refugee comes from," he said, smirking.

"I knew it was a good idea! So, would it have been useful to you, in retrospective?" he asked.

The man nodded in exaggerated agreement. "Oh yes! In so many ways. There were so many things that I had to learn the hard way."

Franz was jittery with excitement. "Like what, for example?"

"Oh wow, where to start…" the man laughed nervously. "So many things…"

Franz had heard enough. He stretched out his arm, preparing for a high five. "I am convinced. Let's do it!" he shouted euphorically.

The pizza baker's smile was now as bright as a light bulb. He reached for the mayor's hand and smacked it as strong as he could.

"Wonderful! And how exactly are we going to do it with the money?"

Franz took a deep breath. "I am known to be a man of my word and of great fairness."

Luigi nodded impatiently.

Franz scratched his beard again. "How about I give you half of the money now and the other half the next time we will see each other? What do you say? Does that sound fair to you?"

The pizza chef could barely contain his delight.

"I will start working right away – boss!" he answered in a sugary tone.

SIX

Although Franz was not a particularly spiritual person, he always had respect for what he could not understand. Growing up in a typical Maislander family, he had been surrounded by sacred and religious items for as long as he could remember. There were crosses and statues of the Virgin Mary and small bottles of holy water scattered around the house and in no particular order. The one item Franz found most fascinating was a large dream catcher, which curiously enough was placed next to the kitchen table on the wall. He once asked his mother why she chose this particular place, and she replied that they were a family of daydreamers and that all they could think about was food anyway.

His late mother, who had died in a freak gardening accident a couple of years before, had an impressive collection of stones and crystals that she would spend hours talking to every night. As a young boy, Franz often wondered what she was on about. 'It's not like they will ever answer you,' he would tell her. But she would just smile as if she knew something he didn't.

Like most other inhabitants of Maisland and of planet earth, Franz was opportunistically religious. He used the Sunday Mass and all other Masses around Christian holidays for village politics and only really visited Father Benedikt when he was in deep trouble or needed advice.

Like every afternoon, the confessional of Maisland's church was open for the community, and after taking a number from the ticket dispenser and waiting almost three hours, it was finally Franz's turn.

"Father Benedikt, it is good to see you again," he whispered.

"My favorite Maislander, come in." The young priest possessed a comically nasal voice.

"I need your help, father Benedikt."

"First of all, go down on your knees, son."

Franz hated that part. Over the years, as his weight increased exponentially, so did the pain in his kneecaps.

"Thanks for seeing me on such short notice, Father," he said.

"Oh, come on, I'm not only your priest but one of your closest friends." The priest sounded like a cartoon snake.

Franz looked up pensive.

"I had this dream. I mean, it was more like a vision," he said, trying to ignore the pain in his knees.

"Tell me more, Fritz."

"It's Franz."

"Yes of course. Franz."

The mayor closed his eyes in reflection. "So, there was this tiny little goat that talked to me. We were both on a red carpet, and Babsi stared straight into my eyes."

"Who is Babsi?" Father Benedikt whispered.

"Babsi is the goat."

"Yes, gotcha."

"So, as I said, Babsi stared me down with these intense green eyes, and it turned out that the eyes were emeralds," Franz continued.

"Wait stop!" The priest was moving around the confessional, his robes rubbing against the walls of the small box.

"Green is the color of the devil; we might have a real problem here," he said with a worried tone. "I hope you still have enough holy water?"

Father Benedikt wasn't your typical priest. His overly large and pointy nose and the dark black tonsure he meticulously waxed day in and day out made him look much more severe than he actually was. To most Maislanders he was a funny, caring, and very engaged member of the community, and although he had a bad reputation when it came to accounting and management of church funds, he was their personal link to the divine, and that was enough to calm down any inquiries and small protests.

Franz himself was also very fond of Benedikt. He had nurtured a good relationship with him ever since he was assigned to the small Maislander church and admired the young priest's strong commitment to the community. As an occasional gambler, Franz would often see Father Benedikt at the local casino, where the priest relentlessly tried to persuade good people to give up gambling. All in all, he was a good person with a big heart. The only thing he could agree with Madame Theresa on, was that, at times, he could be a little too pushy trying to sell his holy water.

"Yes, I do have enough of it. Last time I got the big canister. For that price, I could have bought new tires for my car," Franz said.

Father Benedikt took a long and deep breath.

"I know it is not the cheapest, but it's organic and filled up from the Jordan River in an eco-friendly way," the priest replied.

"I know, I know."

"Continue with your story, son," Father Benedikt said. "I am interested in why this goat demon was talking to you?"

"I don't think it was a demon," Franz said.

The priest coughed in a sarcastic way.

"It gave me advice on how to deal with the refugees coming to Maisland," he continued.

"What did it say?"

"That is why I am here." Franz slid the separator of the confessional open. "I will be creating a manual on how to behave like one of us, so they can integrate easier, and I need your help."

The priest nodded.

"Do you happen to know if they are Christians? I mean, it's such a substantial part of being a Maislander," Franz continued proudly.

Father Benedikt looked up in thought.

"I am not an expert on this matter, but I'm afraid that there is a good chance they are not Christians," the priest said decisively.

Franz opened his mouth in astonishment. He was worried, and for a good reason, but as head of the town, he had to keep a cool head – especially in front of another influential Maislander.

"So, what should we do about it?" he said.

Father Benedikt nodded as if he had the answers to all of their problems and could deliver them on a silver platter.

"There is no doubt that the first thing we should do is baptize them in a lot of holy water. I am not sure if I have enough of it here, but I'm sure that for the right price…"

"Stop it with the holy water!" Franz raised his voice. "I need you to write a chapter for the manual or something."

Father Benedikt frowned.

"Fine, I will help you. But is there a way you can maybe support the church? This month the donations have decreased a lot."

"I'll buy another canister of holy water, alright?" Franz said quickly.

"That is very generous of you. I will let you have the chapter in the next couple of days."

"Thank you, Father."

SEVEN

As he entered Madame Theresa's ice cream parlor, Wolfgang was struck by how much the place looked like a time capsule. Every single item in that shop must have been there since its opening, a couple of decades ago.

The main baronial room, which was supposed to represent a feasting hall in ancient Greece, was surrounded by plastic columns and statues of Greek gods. In the same fashion and with the same pompous style, numerous tables were covering a mosaic looking foil in the center of the room, encircled by golden chairs with very well-worn red velvet seats.

Next to the entrance and on top of the freezer, which displayed a choice of six different flavors of ice cream, hung a few pictures, posters, and certificates. Next to the award for best ice cream in Maisland, signed by

Mayor Franz Bauer, smiled a very young David Hasselhoff in what must have been one of the first Baywatch posters ever printed.

When Madam Theresa spotted the hunting and fishing gear shop owner examining her parlor, she could not believe her eyes. Over the past twenty years, she had seen guests come and go. Some of them were regulars for a while before they suddenly stopped. Others would only come once a month, but at least every month. Every Maislander had at some point found their way into the parlor.

Wolfgang, however, had never walked through that door before.

"Hello Theresa, you got yourself a nice shop here," he said in a friendly voice.

The wind-blown lady with the cigarette in her mouth looked like she had just seen a ghost.

"I especially like Asclepius, Chronos, and Hestia," he continued.

"What?"

"Well, for a good omen, I would suggest you get yourself a statue of Demeter as well!" he continued.

"Oh, the statues, that's what you mean. What is Demeter?" she asked.

"Thanks for the question. Demeter is the Goddess of Harvest and a good omen for any shop owner that seeks financial success!"

Theresa lit up.

"Well. Welcome to my shop. Are you here to eat ice cream?" she asked.

"I am indeed!" he replied with a radiant smile.

"What can I serve you?"

"On average, people order approximately 2.3 scoops of ice cream, is that correct?" he continued.

Madam Theresa nodded, a little perplexed.

"To keep it practical, I will try two scoops!" he announced.

"But if you pay three scoops, the third one is on the house!"

Wolfgang scrunched his face. "That's a very interesting offer."

Madam Theresa smiled pleased. "It's our special spring offer," she said proudly.

"So, what flavors can I get you?"

"Something with very little sugar."

"Perfect! All of my flavors are made with way more milk than sugar. Do you want to eat it here in my beautiful parlor or take away?"

Wolfgang looked around.

"I will have it here if you care to keep me company. I really enjoy the interior."

Madame Theresa made a sign to one of her employees to take over the freezer and walked her newest guest to a table.

"Is it the first time in your life that you're having ice cream?" she asked.

"It is indeed," Wolfgang replied while cautiously inspecting the two scoops of ice cream in the flower-shaped bowl.

"And why is that?"

"Ice cream is very high in sugar, which makes up the majority of its carbohydrate content. Extensive consumption can result in increased levels of blood triglyceride," he said with a lecturing tone.

Madame Theresa shrugged her shoulders. "It's the business I am in."

Wolfgang gave her an understanding look. "Guns are also supposed to be very bad for humans, but I sell them anyway!"

Theresa smiled ingenuously.

"My dear Theresa, you probably heard about the refugee center coming to Maisland. Why do you think people are so mad?" he asked.

The woman seemed absorbed in her thoughts.

"You talk to a lot of people. What do they say?" he continued.

Wolfgang was in no mood for ice cream. He also didn't particularly like the shop and its over-the-top interior, but that didn't really matter. The reason he walked into the parlor was simply to find out what regular Maislanders thought about the refugee center. The more time he had spent with his new comrades of More Guns, Less Refugees, the more he realized that he didn't understand what their anger was all about. Certain aspects of it he could perfectly grasp, but there was an underlying frustration and fear that he just couldn't get his head around. What he needed was the consultation of an expert.

The strangely charming Madame Theresa moved her chair closer to Wolfgang's and placed her hand on his leg in a clumsy movement.

"What I hear from people is that they are scared of refugees," she said, attempting to reproduce a smoky but sensual tone.

Wolfgang flinched, surprised. His cheeks instantly turned red as he stared with wide eyes at Madame Theresa's hand. "That makes sense," he said hesitantly as his voice went up an octave. "I do see how the refugees are not Austrians and as such can be perceived as a threat to the Austrian culture but isn't it ridiculous to think that they would take over our culture?" he continued in a more composed tone.

Madame Theresa shook her head.

"People think that they will take away their jobs, mistreat their wives and daughters, disrespect their culture, vandalize, and so on," she replied, while moving her hand up his leg.

Wolfgang was now radiating like a hot pan.

"Do people really think that all of a sudden all female Maislanders will be forced to wear Hijabs or Burqas?" he stuttered.

"What is a Hijab?"

"Nothing. Forget about it. I just think it's ridiculous."

Madame Theresa moved her hand even further up Wolfgang's leg, deliberately stopping dangerously close to his genital area.

Wolfgang froze. He wished for the earth to open up and swallow him whole.

"Look, in total honesty, I also disagree with them," she said.

"You do?" he asked with a trembling voice.

"Of course, I do. That's ridiculous. They should have the chance to come here, find a job and make our local economy stronger. That way, you will be able to sell more guns, and I will sell more ice cream!" she replied.

Wolfgang backed away just enough to liberate himself from Madame Theresa's hand and from the fervid feeling of embarrassment that had taken over him.

"I'm not sure it's that easy, but yeah, I'll think about it," he said decisively, trying to regain control over his body and mind.

"Why are you asking me all of this? Does it have anything to do with all of those people coming over to your shop in the middle of the night?" she asked.

Wolfgang startled.

"Oh, those meetings?" he said. "No, they're just in preparation for a party I am hosting for the village fair next week," he lied.

"Ah, now that makes sense."

"So, you are hosting a side event to the one organized by the city at the *Festhalle*?" she asked.

Wolfgang sighed.

"I wouldn't call it a side event, it will just be a small get together with my friends and loyal customers," he replied.

Theresa put on her most charming smile. "Do you think it would be possible for me to have a little stand there where I can sell my ice cream? I think it would be a great opportunity to make everybody's day sweeter, what do you say?" she asked.

"Sure, why not." He didn't really care about the stand and told her he had no objections.

"The party will be taking place on my plot of land, next to the sports center," he continued.

The woman almost jumped up from excitement. "The one they offered you a lot of money for to build the refugee center on?" she asked.

"What are you talking about?"

Theresa winked at him. "It's OK, I know you can't tell me," she whispered.

Wolfgang stood, and rearranged his snug cargo shorts.

"Dear Theresa, it has been a pleasure. Many thanks for the ice cream. It was delicious. I have a party to organize now so I hope you'll excuse me," he said.

"Wolfgang, it was so nice of you to stop by. I hope everything was OK with the ice cream, it seems like you barely touched it. Should I prepare you an extra-large box to take away?"

Wolfgang shook his head. "Thanks, but if truth be told, it's not really my thing."

"I understand. If you ever feel like talking again, come see me at my apartment. I have some cashew nuts left," she said with a wink that made him blush all over again.

EIGHT

Pizza Hawaii was not only popular in Goldau but also considered the number one culinary destination in the region. Its opening, ten years ago, had sent shock waves through the entire valley, and every local newspaper and magazine had written about the bold new restaurant.

Berthold, the fearless reporter of the Maisland Bulletin specializing in food, lifestyle, politics, business, health, and horoscopes, was one of the lucky invitees at the VIP opening. He generously wrote: 'Pizza Hawaii is not about the food, it's about the experience - if you can call it that. What I can confirm is that there is absolutely nothing more than meets the eye'.

Girls of the Valley, the regional version of Playboy, had also described it quite floridly: 'You have to be blind not to notice Pizza Hawaii. Its welcoming sign lights up half of Goldau, and when you walk into the place, the pink and green neon lights feel like a hot summer slap in your face'.

Franz had never been there before. Not because he didn't like Pizza but because he tried to avoid visiting the neighboring village of Goldau – especially since Arnold Kraut became Mayor.

As he walked in, however, he regretted not having been a regular guest. The ambiance was warm and welcoming. Palm trees were nestled in every corner, and the colored lights created a slightly trashy but cozy atmosphere. Ukulele music swam through the speakers, lulling him into vacation mode.

As Franz was about to take a place at a wooden table with a mean-looking totem carved into its length, a youngish woman wearing a flower crown approached him.

"Aloha, welcome to Pizza Hawaii" she said, giving him a big fake smile.

The mayor smiled back. There was definitely something exotic about her. Maybe it was the hay-covered skirt she was showing off with great pride, or perhaps just the way she moved, but Franz Bauer was intrigued.

"Here, have a look at the menu," she said.

Franz blushed. He wasn't really hungry, but he definitely didn't want to miss out on a chance to talk to the waitress.

"Can you recommend anything?" he asked.

"Well, we are widely famous for our Pizza Hawaii. It is quite unique because we use fair-trade pineapples from Costa Rica."

Franz grabbed the menu. "Anything else that is special in your restaurant? It is my first time here, so I really don't know what to order."

The waitress gifted him with an adorable smile, this time, it seemed more sincere.

"Oh, I have never met anybody that hasn't been here before. If you don't know our menu at all, I would suggest you have a proper look at it, it's 3D!" she said with great enthusiasm.

As Franz opened the menu, a three-dimensional palm tree emerged from the middle.

"Oh, wow, that is pretty cool, it's like one of those birthday-cards," he said.

The waitress nodded in excitement. "Yes exactly! I still get surprised every time I open it, and that happens like what, fifty times a day?"

"I can imagine. So, what else is typical at Pizza Hawaii? Is the concept like an Italian Hawaiian fusion?" Franz asked.

The waitress winked at him. "You recognized it. A lot of people don't. We must be the first one worldwide," she replied and paused.

"For appetizers, we have our signature Mozzarella alla Waikiki as well as the Surfer's Carpaccio. When it comes to the main courses, you must have the Filetto Mahalo," she continued.

Franz was even more intrigued now. "What is the Surfer's Carpaccio?"

"Oh, it's an ordinary carpaccio, we just serve it on a miniature surfboard."

"OK…and what about the Filetto Mahalo?"

"Yeah, that's also a regular steak. It comes with fries and pineapple jam. The pineapple jam is also fair-trade," she replied.

Franz looked confused. "So why is it called Mahalo? Is it because of the pineapple jam?"

"What? No! It's because Mahalo means thank you in Hawaiian," she replied, slightly irritated.

"OK that makes sense. I think I will have the Pizza Hawaii," Franz said.

"Excellent choice! Do you want it with fair-trade pineapples or regular?"

"I thought you only serve fair-trade pineapple?"

"Nooo, I said we have fair-trade pineapple."

"So, what's the difference between the two?" he asked.

"Around five bucks."

"I'll go with the regular one."

The waitress rolled her eyes. "OK, I'm not judging or anything, but it looks to me like you don't care about the environment."

"I really don't understand what that means," Franz replied. "Could you please tell Luigi that Franz is here?

Maybe he can come to my table once he finishes baking my pizza?"

The waitress nodded curtly.

Franz was befuddled. He couldn't understand how the conversation had turned from friendly borderline flirty to an absolute catastrophe in a matter of minutes.

"You come to my restaurant, and you order a fucking pizza with pineapple?" A strong voice with a thick foreign accent spoke behind Franz's back.

It took the Mayor a couple of seconds to recognize Luigi. The man he had envied for his great style and appealing appearance was wearing a light blue football jersey, white doctor pants, and a chef's skull-cap.

"Luigi, my friend, how are you?"

"What are you doing here?" the pizzaiolo replied with a dry tone.

"Well, I was wondering if you had something for me. The first part of the manual as we agreed," Franz said.

Luigi looked around nervously. "I do, but you can't come to my workplace."

"OK and why is that?"

"Because my boss doesn't want me to talk to customers."

"Wait a second. Is your boss discriminating against you because you are a refugee?" he whispered. "You know I can make one phone call to Berthold at the Maisland Bulletin, and you'll make the front page," he continued.

Luigi shook his head. "No, this isn't about that. Just leave it be."

The cook passed Franz a collection of wrinkled waiter pad sheets. "Here you go! Next time, I will come to your office."

Franz was euphoric. "Thanks a lot, my dear Luigi, I hope you have a great day."

The pizzaiolo gave Franz a severe look. "Enjoy your shitty pizza, and don't ever come back here!"

Franz began to read.

How to become a Maislander
Introduction

This place sucks.
People here suck.
Life here is the absolute worst.

The food is unbelievably bad.
I don't want to get into the details, but they eat pizza with pineapple – that should say it all. I know I said that I wouldn't get into the details, but there are a couple of things you absolutely need to know. Besides terrible pizza, I have the feeling that everything they eat is either deep-fried or swims in hefty sauces. You will have stomach problems at first, but your body will get used

to it eventually. At least, I hope so. I still get the occasional attack of diarrhea, mostly related to the tons of sour cream they generously spread all over half of their dishes.

Let me see what else I can tell you...
The weather is also extremely dreadful. At least a hundred and fifty days throughout the year, you will want to kill yourself. The village and the whole valley are just so depressing that all you wish for is to jump from a seven-story building. And here you'll encounter the next problem: there is no building higher than three stories. You will have to make use of a hunting rifle. It's not the most relaxed way to go, but I guess very effective.

The rest of the year, except for the month of July and half of August, you will be in a constant state of advanced melancholy. You will remember your hometown, your friends, and family with great sadness, and you won't be shy of shedding tears. It's very sad, I know, but that's just the way it is.

As I mentioned before - the people here - are horrifying. They have everything in life except for warmth, compassion, a sense of humor, and, more generally, emotions. When they have an issue with you, they would never ever mention it to you. Their preferred *way of dealing with their passive-aggressiveness is to complain about you to other people, especially friends that you might have in common. In a second step, those same friends would then tell you about the complaints they have just heard from your friend, but only if you promise them not to tell him/her that they told you. In a third step, what usually happens is that when you finally decide to confront that person with what you heard from your mutual friends, they would usually deny everything and tell you that everything is fine and that they love you.*

Truth is, I still don't understand why you decided to come here, and truly I could say the same thing about me, but now you are here, so let's try to make the best out of it.
I hope with this manual, I can help you survive in this jungle of sadness and depression.

In the following chapters, I will guide you through this dreadful experience and will try to make your life a little less miserable.

Enjoy the read.

NINE

Dear Franz,

I have not received an answer to my first letters yet. Are you too busy?

Anyway, I have something to report to you.
Believe it or not, Wolfgang came into the ice cream parlor yesterday. He said he had never had ice cream before, and he wanted to try some. And you want to hear the best thing about it? He pretended to be interested in my life and started asking me a lot of questions. Most of them were about the refugee center and how people felt about it.

You know how he thinks he is so much smarter than everybody else? Well, yesterday, I think he got a taste of his own medicine. As I said, while he was trying to be so polite and asking a hundred questions, I managed to turn the tables and asked him about his recent dealings. Well, it turns out his late-night meetings were in preparation for next week's village fair. He is organizing a parallel event to your party at the Festhalle. But he did offer me the chance to set up an ice cream stand – would you be prepared to do the same? Rent-free?

Also, I had the pleasure of talking to father Benedikt yesterday!
As I walked into the church, I was already prepared to decline any special offer to buy holy water, but then I saw him sitting by the big cross with blank pages spread all over the altar. Turns out, he is writing a chapter for a manual for the refugees coming to Maisland. Now he didn't tell me why or for whom, but I guess it is coming from you? If yes, could you please include this passage?

"Ice cream is one of the most important meals in our culture. There is a misconception that one can only eat it in summer or when it's warm outside – I have never heard anything more wrong! Ice cream contains a lot of milk, which is good for your bones. In Maisland, the number one ice cream parlor is without a doubt Madame Theresa's. This season she will have six different flavors, including lemon, which has a high content of vitamin C. Where else can you find such a selection?

Experts suggest having at least one, but preferably two ice creams a day. Most parlors, including Madame Theresa's, have loyalty programs, like buy 40 and get one free. Also, please note that Madame Theresa's parlor is the only one in the valley (no responsibility is accepted for the accuracy of this information)."

A bubbly kiss from my bathtub ;)
Theresa

TEN

When Franz entered the church from its extravagant main entrance, it was already early evening. Most Maislanders were at home finishing up a light dinner. In Maisland, the main meal of the day is lunch. That's when all the housewives give their best in the kitchen to satisfy their hard-working husbands. By dinner, their energy is spent, and all they can muster up are a couple of slices of dark bread with butter and cheese.

After inspecting every corner of the church in what turned out to be an unsuccessful attempt to locate father Benedikt, he took the back exit to the church's garden. In a remote corner, hidden behind two large memorial stones, he spotted the priest filling up what seemed to be holy water canisters with a water hose.

"Father Benedikt, here you are," Franz said.

The priest jumped up in surprise.

"Oh, hello Fritz, good to see you," he replied nervously.

Franz stepped closer. "What are you doing with the holy water canisters?" He pointed at several empty canisters located right next to the priest

"These canisters?" Father Benedikt replied. "Oh, well." The Priest caressed his forehead. "These are empty canisters that I use to water the flowers. You see, once a canister with holy water is emptied, it cannot be reused. It loses its power," he continued.

Franz sighed in relief. "That's what I thought. It just looked like you were filling up canisters with regular water before selling it as holy water."

"No, no, I would never do such thing!"

"Anyway, I am here for the manual, have you finished your part?" Franz asked.

"Sure, sure. Please take a seat on the bench, I'll go to my office and get it."

The church park looked a lot like the Garden of Eden. The grass was soft and well-cut, and in summer, cherry and apple trees colored the surroundings like an impressionist painting while offering shade to a couple of wooden benches.

Although the place looked like it was right out of the Book of Genesis, it was the most feared site in the whole valley. Some people argued that it was exactly because of its pure and idyllic appearance that it had to be haunted. Most Maislanders even referred to it as the graveyard, which obviously caused a lot of confusion – especially when it came to funerals.

Maisland's church was a gothic masterpiece, dating back to the 12th century, but it was only in recent history that a garden was added to the church grounds. In the year 1975, it was Father Johannes that, under the guidance of the Mayor at the time, Michael Meyer, decided to bless the garden and transform it into a sacred church park.

Rumor says that Father Johannes didn't have a good feeling about it from the start. The day he performed the ritual, the very same trees that are still standing strong on the edges of the park today, were overloaded with ravens. The birds stood there, firmly anchored to the branches, crowing loudly until the ceremony was over, and then they all flew off, the sky a mass of black. On July 2nd of the same year, the first disaster occurred. The daughter of Mayor Michael Meyer had asked Father Johannes to host her wedding ceremony in the park, and being the daughter of the Mayor, the priest quickly agreed and even organized the construction of an extraordinarily large wooden cross to be placed behind the altar. Halfway into the ceremony, on a perfect summer day under the bluest sky imaginable, lightning struck the cross. The bride, groom, and another six guests were killed instantly, and another four people suffered concussions. After the incident, Father Johannes, who miraculously survived, made it his mission to not allow anybody to use the park for anything that was somehow church-related.

In the spring of 2015, just as Father Benedikt had been assigned to Maisland, a young couple from Goldau approached him and requested their wedding be held in the beautiful park behind the church. The priest did his homework and found out that the garden was indeed sacred ground and that it wouldn't be a problem holding the ceremony there. While researching, he was warned several times about what happened in 1975 but decided to ignore the words and write it off as a freak accident. Although it did seem a little suspect that the couple had agreed to buy three hundred little bottles of holy water for their guests.

On August 3rd, 2015, the second disaster took place. Towards the end of the magical ceremony, the area in the center of the garden, where all the guests were seated in white cane chairs, suddenly collapsed, and everybody fell into a hole that measured thirteen meters deep – although this was only a guess as no one would agree to go near it. It was the biggest tragedy the valley had ever seen, and all the neighboring villages decided to hold a remembrance ceremony. Madame Theresa had offered her parlor for the event, with a ten percent discount if you ordered more than four scoops. For Father Benedikt, it also turned out to be a lesson he had to learn the hard way. He embraced his mistake and made it his mission to only accept pre-payment for holy water in the future.

"You think we will be fine sitting on this bench?" Franz asked nervously as the priest handed him a single page of what seemed to be ancient papyrus.

Father Benedikt tapped his shoulder. "My friend, I was here the day the disaster happened, and I still come every day, so don't worry," he replied.

Franz sighed in relief and made the sign of the cross.

The priest jumped up. "What are you doing, are you crazy?" he shouted at Franz.

"Why? What did I do?"

"Don't make religious signs, don't you know what happened here?" he shouted. "A lot of people died, have a bit of respect!"

Franz shifted on his seat and glanced around. He didn't feel safe at all.

"It's ok, that's why I'm here. My job is to guide you, my Maislander," the priest said.

"Anyway, read my chapter. It's not very long, but it's very insightful."

Religion in Maisland

My dear future Maislander, I have done my research, and I am pretty confident that if you are reading this, you are a Muslim. I am not judging you for this. It is not my place to judge. I am sure somebody is though if you know what I mean.

Anyway, Maisland is a proudly Catholic village, and you should be aware of that.

In case you are not familiar with Christianity, we believe in one god - so actually, just like you (as far as what I read is correct). The house of our God, where we meet on a regular basis, is called the Church - if I am not mistaken in your religion, a similar thing would be a Mosque? Now, it is clear to me that you must be very much attached to your religion and your rituals, and so are we. Since you decided to move here to Maisland, however, I think that it would be more appropriate for you to adapt to our way of things instead of all of us adapting to yours – I hope you understand.

The first step hereby would be for you to accept that Jesus was, in fact, crucified. I mean, thinking that he wasn't - even for a split second - makes me unwell in my stomach. I know for a fact that you acknowledge his existence, which I guess is something already. Now, in a nutshell, what can the Christian church offer you that Islam can't? Very simple, my friend from very far: salvation. Jesus paid for our sins already, so that we are guaranteed salvation, doesn't that sound good to you? If I was you, I would definitely consider joining the cool cats of the Catholic Church.

To conclude, I have been made aware that in this manual, I should not emphasize the importance of holy water too much. Nonetheless, there is NOTHING as such in your religion, and having such a key role in finding success in life, feel free to contact me in case you are interested. If needed, I can make home delivery too, also in the middle of the night. And you can pay with credit card.

Spiritually yours,
Father Benedikt

Franz folded the document in two. "Look Father, I have no idea if what you wrote is true, but I like the fact that it's short, clear, and informative," he said.

The priest nodded.

"The only thing I need to ask you is to please leave out the conclusion. I don't think it's nice to give them a manual that encourages them to buy something - that is not the right message!"

Father Benedikt was still nodding, but in a disappointed way.

"Okay I understand your point, my dear," the priest said.

"Thank you! Could you please let me have the final version in the next couple of hours?"

"Sure Fritz, anything for you."

ELEVEN

Something just didn't seem right with the *Festhalle*. And it wasn't so much that it was made out of plaster and was about a hundred times smaller than the original one, there was something wrong with its proportions. The actual event location was a clear rectangle, and the outline of the model was undeniably a square.

"Who built this?" Franz asked.

Jenny scratched her head. "I did. Is there something wrong with it?"

"Is there something wrong with it?" Franz pulled his young secretary closer to the model. "Have you ever been to the *Festhalle*? Because this doesn't look like it at all!"

"Yes, of course I have been there," she replied snidely.

Franz huffed and puffed out lout. "Well, obviously you have, it was a rhetorical question."

"So, what's wrong with it?" she asked.

"The outline…it's a square!"

Jenny lifted the roof from the model. "Come on Franz, it's just a model. What is important is what is inside."

Franz sent her a gracious smile. "You are right, I am sorry. I'm just so stressed right now. I would love to put all of my energy into the village fair and all of the attractions we will have, but the refugee center, the manual, and the elections in three weeks…I'm trying to keep my head above water. You have been doing an amazing job coordinating the fair - I shouldn't be lashing out at you like that."

Jenny stared at him blankly.

"Thank you so much, my dear Jenny. Shall we start with the inside of the location? What do you have for me?" Franz continued.

"Sure!" Her smile this time was radiant. "On the main stage inside of the *Festhalle* we will have a band playing the whole night and…"

"Which band?" Franz interrupted her.

"Well, they are not really famous, but they make good rock music. In addition to the band, in front of the stage, we will have a…"

"Which band?" he interrupted her again.

Jenny took a deep breath. "Skirt Hunters," she murmured.

Franz started coughing heavily as if he had just swallowed a mouthful of hot coffee into his trachea.

"You got to be kidding me," he howled.

Skirt Hunters were the most famous and, at the same time, infamous rock band in the valley. What was most interesting about them was that they had an extremely polarizing effect on people, you either loved and worshipped them or hated them with an equal if not greater amount of passion – there was no in-between. Most of their extraordinarily loyal fans had multiple tattoos of the band's logo – a telescope reaching under a skirt – and listened exclusively to their music, in their trucks, homes, and on their CD players. In most bars of Maisland and Goldau, you would often hear their most famous single 'A Skirt Can Never Be Too Short' over and over again.

On the other hand, people that hated Skirt Hunters hated them to the extent that is usually reserved for pedophiles and human traffickers. The anger and aggression the band unleashed in certain individuals were so intense that they had to start moving around incognito. Their old tour bus, which had a large version of their logo printed on both sides, had been shot at more than a dozen times, had its tires continuously slashed, and was set on fire twice.

Although their music was quite unique and objectively pleasant, it still clearly divided listeners. To some, their mix of nostalgic American rock of the eighties and nineties and traditional Austrian folk music represented a match made in heaven, while to others, it was a laxative taken in through the ears. Reviews of the band members varied way from the sexiest man in the valley to STD-stuffed raccoon. The truth was that all four of them were well beyond their forties, wore hair and clothing that had not been modern since *Flashdance* came out, and were still waiting in vain for their big breakthrough.

Franz obviously hated them and their vulgar logo, especially because he got to contemplate it every day on Jenny's ankle.

"Are you serious? After what they pulled last year?" he continued.

Inhabitants of Maisland were still talking about the aftermath of their performance during last year's village fair. The band's tour manager had taken proper precautions before their show and distributed earplugs to people that were complaining already before the band even got on stage and managed to forbid the circulation of glasses and glass bottles. The result was that Skirt Hunters delivered a solid performance without major interruptions or injuries and decided to celebrate the occasion by drinking 120 Jägermeister shots. What happened next varies depending on who one asks. The lead singer allegedly stole a donkey from a nearby farm and rode it all the way to Goldau to have a drunken meal at Pizza Hawaii. The guitarist, who arguably generated the most damage and confusion, manipulated the mechanics of the Ferris wheel well beyond its top speed, resulting in dozens of people puking and three of them being catapulted out of the gondolas. Fortunately, nobody was seriously injured, but the attraction was completely destroyed, resulting in hundreds of thousands in property damage. On a less dramatic note, the drummer ended up in bed with Jenny and her male cousin.

Franz massaged his temples. "I can't believe you booked them again!"

Jenny looked at him with puppy eyes. "I'm sorry, but I am dating one of the guys now. What am I supposed to do?"

"OK fine, but you keep an eye on them. No alcohol for the whole band, and especially not for that crazy guitarist. We are still paying for that wheel. I am sure you know that," Franz replied with a patronizing tone.

Jenny stretched out her hand. "Promise!"

"What else do we have inside of the *Festhalle*?"

"In front of the main stage, in the right corner, we'll have a Jägermeister bar. In the left corner, there will be a beer stand, sponsored by Pilsner's Hell, and in the middle, I managed to make space for Theresa's ice cream stand," Jenny replied.

"Thanks for squeezing in, Theresa. I'm sure that a lot of guests will enjoy a cold ice cream in between a pint of beer and a shot of Jäger."

"Yeah, that makes absolute sense," Jenny replied, smirking in that way she reserved for people who didn't get things.

"What do we have for the outside?" Franz asked.

"Well, as you can imagine, this year, we will not have a Ferris wheel."

Franz nodded.

"What we do have is the shooting game, facilitated once more by Wolfgang, a punching ball, the milk-cans stand, the mirror maze, and of course the legendary ghost train."

Franz seemed pleased with the range of entertainment stations. "That sounds very good. We just have to keep an eye on the shooting game. Do you remember what happened two years ago, when the elders started to fire their real rifles?" Franz said, rubbing his face.

Jenny shook her head affirmatively. "Yes, and we should have a closer look at the ghost train. Last year, some of the elders fell asleep on the train and rode it for multiple hours, not making space for any other visitors to enjoy."

"Okay, it looks like everything is taken care of. Is there anything else from your side, Jenny?"

"I have been asking around about Wolfgang's side event. Especially because he is hosting the shooting game at our event."

"You are right, I almost forgot, Wolfgang the special snowflake. What are people saying?" Franz asked.

"Well, surprisingly, nobody is saying anything!"

"What do you mean? This is Maisland, when has it ever happened that nobody had anything to say?"

"It almost looks like he hasn't planned anything yet."

"OK, I'll ask around." Franz walked back to his chair. "Oh yeah, I have one more thing to ask you. Have you seen Father Benedikt? I have been trying to reach him all day, it seems like he disappeared from the face of the earth."

Jenny took out an envelope from the back pocket of her jeans. "I have no idea. I don't really go to church and quite honestly, Father Benedikt just creeps the shit out of me." She paused as if waiting for a reaction from Franz, but he gave her nothing.

"Anyway, I have a letter for you from my mom – again. Please let me know if I should tell her to stop writing you."

"As a matter of fact, thank her for all her letters. I haven't had the chance to reply yet. Now go home and rest. You'll need a lot of energy for the fair."

Dear Franz,

I have quite good news for once.
We finally managed to get rid of Father Benedikt!

I don't know if you heard what happened, but after a long investigation by the police, it turned out that our beloved priest was a degenerate gambler. Over the past four years, apparently, he lost a couple of millions playing roulette at the casino.

Where did he get the money from, you may ask? Well, the police say that he basically emptied the church's accounts. But that's not all. Contacts of mine, who spend way more time than me gossiping, told me that Father Benedikt was also the head of a smuggling and counterfeiting ring. Shocker: the holy water he sold for a couple of hundreds a bottle was nothing more than rainwater.

I feel truly sorry for all those idiots that bought all that water the past years – and it must be quite the number considering the fact that he gambled away millions.
As I said, I feel truly sorry for them and I hope that now, instead of spending money on useless water, they come over to the parlor a bit more often.

I'm creating brand new flavors for the summer, including Vanilla and Coconut. Do you think I'm being too adventurous? Last year I had to explain to every customer what a mango was, and that was not ideal, especially because I also had no clue what it was. I still don't.

Anyway, you know me, I put any ice-cream flavor in my mouth ;)

L.O.V.E.
Theresa

TWELVE

A couple of drops of sweat had already materialized on Franz's forehead.

"I really don't feel comfortable," he murmured.

Standing by the door in front of him was Luigi, surrounded by four hostile-looking chaperones.

The pizza chef from Goldau smiled at him sardonically. "How come you don't feel comfortable? They are all cousins of mine," he replied, indicating his entourage.

Although the mayor didn't know the reason behind this unexpected appointment, he was ready to bet all of what he had that this was no pleasure visit.

The men around Luigi were a heterogeneous mix of heights, hair, beard length, and density, as well as various skin tones. What they all had in common, however, was an unmistakably shady look and flashy gold chains hanging from their necks and embedded in their hairy chests, which due to some terrible fashion faux pas, were exposed.

Franz was close to hyperventilating. "I understand. They just look very intimidating," he replied.

The pizzaiolo from Goldau burst out laughing. "Intimidating? Come on. They are the nicest guys on the planet!" he roared.

Franz recoiled in his chair. "I mean look at the tiny guy," Franz nodded at the one close to the door with a strangely slim mustache. "He is clearly holstering a gun in his waistband - I mean, it's not even hidden under his shirt. It's just there, for anybody to see."

The small man instantly jumped forward and reached for his gun. "Who did you call tiny, you piece of shit? Do you want to die? I'm going to make your kids disappear," he shrieked.

"What kids?"

Luigi raised his hand. "Relax, relax he didn't mean it that way, am I right?" he said, sending a penetrating look the mayor's way.

Franz nodded. "Yes of course I meant it in the nicest way possible, obviously!"

"There you go. So, tell me mayor, how did you like the introduction to the manual?" Luigi asked.

Franz looked at the four men again and came to the swift conclusion that this was definitely not the right time for some heroic honesty.

"It was good. I mean I would have liked a bit more of a positive spin. I just felt that it was a little cold, to be completely honest," he said.

Luigi flared his nostrils. "Honesty has no temperature, my dear mayor."

Franz nodded. "And I absolutely get that. Fair enough. Would you be offended if I adapted it just a little to what I had in mind?" Franz asked.

"As long as I get my money, you might as well burn it. But if I don't get my money, you will be the one burning," Luigi said and instantly laughed at his own joke, as did his cousins.

Franz joined them in a laugh. "That's exactly what I expected from you guys. Especially from the short one, he looks really mean," he said, trying hard to extend the joyous and teasing atmosphere.

The laughter died out instantly, and the short man flared up. "Motherfucker, did you call me short again? I will kill you and feed you to the pigs. And then I'll come for your kids. I know where they go to school," he screeched, this time sounding like a hysterical monkey.

Luigi jumped in. "No shit Sherlock, there's one school in the whole valley, where the fuck else would they go?"

Franz coughed out loud in an attempt to deescalate the situation. "I still don't have kids. But I'm very sorry. I didn't mean to call you short again, I just don't know your name, that's why."

The man regained his composure. "Luigi," he replied.

"Great, that makes things easier," Franz rolled his eyes.

"Enough with this bullshit, I came to get the second half of my money," the original Luigi said.

"But we had a deal, my friend. You were supposed to deliver me something before I give you the money?"

"Oh yeah, you are right." The cook retrieved a folded piece of paper out of the pocket of his jeans and threw it on Franz's table. "Here is the bibliography!"

Franz nodded. "Very well, I'm known to be a man of my word," he said and instantly pushed a button on his desk phone. "Jenny, get Luigi the other half of his money!" he barked into the receiver.

The pizzaiolo from Goldau smiled wolfishly at Franz. "Very good, it was a pleasure doing business with you, mayor."

"When can I expect the rest of the manual?" Franz asked.

"Very soon, my friend, very soon!" Luigi replied with a sly look.

"Hasta la vista baby!" the tiny Luigi added.

How to become a Maislander

Introduction

Chapter 1: Maisland: we are screwed, but at least we're in the same boat.

Chapter 2: The weather: remedies for advanced depression.

Chapter 3: The people: how to leave your emotions out of it.

Chapter 4: The food: tricks and tips on how to avoid gushing from both ends.

Chapter 5: Hobbies: how to give them up.

Chapter 6: Employment: driving a tractor and working the land.

Chapter 7: Religion: don't trust the local priest.

Chapter 8: Intoxication: how to have your first beer before 10am.

Chapter 9: Traveling: how to freeze your curiosity.

Conclusion

THIRTEEN

The interrogation room of the Maisland police department resembled a household garage. The main reason for this uncanny resemblance was that it was, in fact, located in the garage of the police department.

Officer Günther Frank, the newest addition to the Maisland Police Department, had made it clear to his colleagues that he was not willing to interview suspects at his desk, surrounded by colleagues, secretaries, and all possible distractions and had therefore requested the funds to build a state-of-the-art interrogation room with the signature one-way mirror and around the clock cameras. Needless to say, his requests were denied.

Being stubborn as usual, he decided to take the bull by the horns and build an interrogation room in the garage of the police department with his own two hands.

Since his early days at Maisland's Alfons Haider elementary, Günther knew he wanted to be in law enforcement. As a young boy, he was not a great student, nor was he particularly gifted in sports. What he did have – however - was a tireless appetite for justice. Before becoming the incarnation of political correctness and moral justice at the police academy, in school, his most notable achievements included ending the careers of three teachers, two kitchen aids, one janitor, and principal Schumacher. In most cases, he had uncovered abuses of power and immoral relationships with students and fellow staff members, but when it came to the wrongdoings of principal Schumacher, he had walked the extra mile. The evidence Günther had gathered illustrated the principal's shady connections to a Burmese Shaman, to the head coach of the Lebanese Olympic Curling Team, and to an empty bank account at the Panama Fidelity Group. The scandal was so outrageous that it even reached beyond the borders of the Maisland Bulletin, making it to page three of Austria's largest newspaper.

As a guarantor for authority and champion of integrity, he never enjoyed much appreciation from his peers. Although he knew that he couldn't have expected much from his classmates at Alfons Haider, he was very disappointed by his comrades' commitment at the police academy. Instead of finding partners, supporters, and enthusiasts for his fight for justice, he was ridiculed and marginalized. Even teachers and superiors disliked him. After graduation, instead of receiving a prestigious position in the capital, he was sent back to Maisland, the only police station that was forced to take him and where nobody wanted to go anyway.

Being a known face and indirectly related to half of Maisland's police force, his first years back in his hometown as a junior officer were marked by his signature appetite for lawfulness. At first, the other officers despised him because of his values and determination. In a police station reigned by boredom, laziness, and bureaucracy, an over-motivated and over-committed new officer doesn't stand a chance. As time passed, however, they started to appreciate him a little. They realized that they had found someone that was not afraid to put in the extra hours to finish reports, patrol town, control traffic, and respond to emergencies. His attention to detail had become so infamous in the valley that citizens had even abstained from reporting a stolen sheep or bicycle, out of fear of being put under the microscope.

"Well, well, well, who would have thought you would be sitting here one day." The young officer took off his Ray-Ban aviator sunglasses and hung them on his shirt pocket.

"Cigarette?" he asked, throwing a pack of red Marlboros on the table.

The man sitting in front of him gazed in confusion.

"You know I don't smoke. And neither do you. Do you think this is a TV show?" he chuckled.

Günther clenched his hands above his head. "You're going away for a long time Father," he declared.

Father Benedikt stared down at his own hands. The metal of the cuffs had already left marks on his wrists. "For what?" he asked, tapping his fingers on the table.

The police officer pushed his chest out. "Come on Father, you know exactly why. I talked to the casino, and they were so kind as to send me your player profile."

The priest crossed his arms and leaned back in his chair, a smug look on his face. "So, I lost a little money gambling; why is that such a big deal?"

"A little money? You lost over two million in less than five years," Günther said calmly.

"I come from a rich family and saved up my salary the last years, is that a crime?" he replied.

"Come on, Father. That is such bullshit. I looked into the church accounts. According to your books, you renovated the church's roof twice and bought a Caravaggio painting."

The priest had trouble keeping eye contact.

"And if that is not enough, I also had the pleasure of talking to your good friend the Baptist last week."

Father Benedikt jumped up. "He is alive?" he asked nervously.

Günther's eyebrows contracted. "Yes, of course, he is alive. Why wouldn't he be?"

The priest breathed a sigh of relief.

"I thought he was dead. He got involved with a powerful bishop of the Orthodox Church. Tried to sell him an enormous amount of fake holy water and got caught. Hadn't heard anything from him for months, so I thought he was dead."

"Well, if it makes you feel better, he is not dead. We arrested your partner a couple of months ago."

Father Benedikt sealed his hands in prayer. "Thank you, god!" he whispered.

"But he did turn on you and went on record with all your dealings." Günther Frank continued.

The priest slammed his hands on the table. "That piece of shit!" he shouted as his veins throbbed in his neck. His partner of so many years had sold him out to the cops. "Why didn't they just kill him…" he murmured.

"You see, my dear Father; the ice is getting thinner and thinner."

"So why did you bring me in then? You have everything on me already. Do you just want to embarrass me? Why not just leave me in custody until trial."

"As much as I enjoy looking into the eyes of a criminal that has been brought to justice, unfortunately, that is not the reason I brought you here."

The priest tried to stare him down with his dusty grey eyes.

"There is something fishy going on in Maisland. This whole refugee center leaves a bad taste in my mouth.

Why would the mayor want to build something like that?" he asked.

The priest shrugged.

"I mean, this must be a case of corruption. Why would Mayor Franz Bauer do something like that of his own free will?"

Father Benedikt shook his head. "This goes way beyond my pay grade. I have no clue…"

Günther nodded. "As you wish. Enjoy your time behind bars. You will have plenty of it to talk to your new best friend, God!"

FOURTEEN

The village fair was one of Franz's favorite events of the year. Even before he became mayor and was sucked into the bureaucracy of politics and the organization of the event, it was one of the highlights of his youth and young adulthood. At times, he even missed those days when he was just one of the many guests, with no responsibilities and years away from being in the public eye.

Founded almost three hundred years earlier, Maisland's most important event was not only a significant day for every inhabitant of the town, but also for most of their neighbors of the surrounding villages. Although in the past the fair had successfully adapted to the trends of the twenty-first century and the entertainment needs of modern society, Franz had made it his task to preserve its traditional elements. His commitment made sure that while food trucks could sell Hawaiian poke bowls, the Maisland fire department was still able to conduct their long-established parade. This approach of blending modernity with tradition proved itself to be highly successful, and the attendance rate had grown exponentially over the last years.

Fueled by the certainty of success and distracted by pre-election preparations, Franz had not put any effort into promoting this year's event. The Maisland's Bulletin refused to publish anything related to the event – not even an entry into their calendar because the Mayor's office had been completely negligent about advertising and financial donations. Among the other unhappy victims of the sudden cut in the marketing budget was local influencer Gabriel Garten, who had become a regional star after being the December boy in an older edition of the farmer's calendar. His rise to fame was the epitome of a modern Cinderella story. Shortly after publishing the nation-wide calendar, the young Maislander was almost instantly catapulted from his uncle's barn to catwalks in small to medium-sized malls. As a glamorous fashion model with a notable amount of followers on his social media pages, he had flirted for a long time with the idea of transitioning from modeling to influencing. Finally, it was his agent who convinced him to give up the photoshoots and dedicate his time to selling his followers merchandise and promoting events.

Due to a recent plunge in revenue from his social-media related income, Gabriel Garten was so upset about the missed earnings from the village fair that he had even addressed the issue publicly in a post that was shared over twenty thousand times.

I will not be attending this year's village fair.
They are still using plastic cups and cutlery, and I really
don't like the way they are treating minorities, animals,
plants, the ocean, and the LGBT community.

BTW I will be attending the 10th anniversary of Pizza
Hawaii next week. Free hugs for all.
Order your pizza online now on: www.pizzahawaiigol-
dau.at

XOXO
Gabriel

As Franz reached the parking lot of the *Festhalle*, ready to make his great entrance, he couldn't believe his eyes. The whole area, which was supposed to be occupied by the fair attractions and food trucks, was completely deserted.

There was only one person in the distance: Berthold. The courageous reporter of the Maisland Bulletin was sitting on a chair at the entrance of the *Festhalle*, dressed in a tailor-made traditional Austrian leather outfit.

Franz ran towards the friendly face of the reporter.

"Hello Berthold, how good to see you. Are you ready for a big party?" Franz asked nervously and a little out of breath.

The full-time painter and part-time reporter looked around for quite a long time before replying. "Yeah sure, I'm super excited. When do you think people will be coming? It looks like I'm the first one."

Franz's jaw dropped. "What do you mean the first one? I'm sure there are a couple of people inside the *Festhalle*?"

"Nope!"

"How is that possible? I'm sure that some fans of the band are there." Franz said.

"What band?" Berthold quickly replied.

"You know those idiots from Skirt Hunters?"

Berthold lit up. "Oh, I love Skirt Hunters, especially their song 'Why can't I pet your pussy'," he said.

Franz made a grimace.

"Well, they are not here," Berthold continued.

Franz turned from confused to utterly worried. "OK let me have a quick look inside. I'm sure it'll be full here in no time."

Behind the entrance doors, where the shot bar was supposed to be handing out generous portions of herbal liquor, stood nothing. Not even a table with a couple of beer cans.

Fueled by a good dose of rage, he took out his phone.

"Jenny! Where the hell are you?"

"Hello, hello, can you hear me?" Jenny replied with loud music blasting in the background.

"Yes I can, where the hell are you?"

His assistant performed an over-exaggerated cough. "I'm at home and not feeling too well."

"What do you mean you're not feeling too well? What about our event?" he screeched.

"Yeah, I'm sorry about that, I think I caught something."

"And what about Skirt Hunters? Where the hell are they? Nobody is here!"

"Oh yeah, I forgot to tell you about that. They canceled yesterday."

A vein popped out of Franz's neck. "You got to be kidding me! Why the hell did they cancel?"

"I think they are playing at some other event."

"What other event?"

"I don't know..." Jenny replied.

Franz felt rage run through his body. "What is that music in the background? Where are you?"

"I'm at home. Sorry for the noise, I have the TV running in the background."

Franz gritted his teeth. "If you are lying to me, I swear I will fire you!"

Jenny coughed.

"Let me ask you once more, where the hell are you?"

He heard two shrill noises, and then the connection was lost.

Franz was fuming. He was so livid he threw his phone to the other end of the *Festhalle* and stormed out.

"Berthold! You are the most notorious reporter of the valley; do you happen to know of any other event in the area?"

Berthold caressed his beard. "I am not sure. I mean, I heard about Wolfgang's event, but apart from that, I really have no idea."

"But Wolfgang's event is more like a friendly thing, no? I doubt that a lot of people went there."

"Yeah, that's what I thought. But the past couple of days, I heard about some crazy attractions that he supposedly set up," Berthold answered.

"What kind of attractions?"

"I'm not sure. But I assume his shooting game and maybe more."

"But how would they all fit into the courtyard of his shop?"

Berthold shook his head. "Not this year, pal. Apparently, he is hosting the party on the piece of land he has next to the sports center."

"That's a huge ass piece of land."

Berthold nodded.

"Do you know of anybody that could be there right now?"

"I am sure Theresa is there. She wouldn't give up the chance to sell ice cream." Berthold replied.

"OK let's call her!" Franz said.

"Sure. I left my phone in the car so I could have a few hours of peace. You must have her number."

Franz did have her number... in his smashed phone inside the *Festhalle*.

FIFTEEN

Dear Franz,

I am writing to you knowing that you must be devastated by what happened at the village fair, and just to make clear, this is not an attempt to rub it in your face or to deliver to you a more than deserved, "I told you so." You know that it is not my style to come back at people this way.

To start off, I would like to apologize for not attending your event at the Festhalle. Also, I'm really sorry that I was not able to send anybody to take care of my stand, but all of my employees were working overtime at Wolfgang's event (not that it really mattered because there was nobody at the Festhalle to buy ice cream anyway). I myself did obviously not attend his event - in case you were wondering. I was extremely busy. I would never do that to you.

Now, let me just quickly report to you what happened at Wolfgang's party (as told to me by my staff).

If I had to describe the event in one word, that word would be: mind-blowing. I mean you should have been there, the attractions, the food, the people – wow, what a show.

Somebody told me that you had originally booked that scum band Skirt Hunters and that they decided last second to cancel on you and perform their horrifying music at Wolfgang's event, is that true? If that is the case, then I must say that your new enemy did an amazing job in handling them. Now get this, you know how Skirt Hunters, who in my eyes and ears are so unbelievably despicable, have quite the fan base here in Maisland (including my very own brain-dead daughter). Well, Wolfgang had the great idea to set up a soundproof tent so they could play their mind-numbing music without disturbing everyone. Meanwhile, for the main stage, outside, he booked Hansi Leatherpants. Let me just say, and I can't keep emphasizing it, Hansi is so unbelievably charming. I know he is in his sixties, but the way his butt is squeezed into those leather pants is just…

Anyway, the rest of the attractions were also super diverse and fun, you could really tell that somebody put a lot of planning and passion into the event. The stand that received the most attention was Wolfgang's own shooting game. This year, instead of having deer and foxes pasteboards as moving targets, he introduced pictures of migrant ships and mosques. Apparently, he ran out of ammunition within the first two hours. I personally found it very disturbing and offensive – you know how I feel about the center and migrants in general. Maislanders should really reconsider their stance, aren't we all migrants if we go far enough back?

The food yard, on the other hand, was probably the best culinary experience I have ever had. In theory, of course, because as I said, I wasn't there. There was this Asian dish with rice and fish, I think it was called shusi or shushi, and it was just delicious – especially towards the end of the fair when the sun had heated up the fish a little bit, and it was no longer so cold. Another delicious thing was a sandwich with hot meat and lettuce. I think the meal was a traditional Arab dish because the guy preparing it had darker skin and was cutting the meat from a large rotating chunk of lamb with a saber. It looked like one of those swords from the movie Aladdin, very fascinating. But please, don't take my word for it. He had a thick mustache, so he might have been Italian, actually.

While I was checking on my staff, I met this very charming young man. I think his name was Gabriel and he is some sort of celebrity because young girls kept taking pictures of him. I decided to hire him to shoot a couple of new posters for the parlor. I was thinking of having him pose naked in front of the ice-cream fridge, with a very big cone covering his private parts – what do you think?

To conclude I would like to tell you about my ice cream stand. My dear Franz, in over twenty years of spreading joy and happiness with my delicious ice cream, I have never had such a successful day. I sold as much product as I would usually do in two weeks – it was crazy. People also seemed to enjoy the newest coconut flavor, which was very surprising to me. All in all, it was a superb experience. I am looking forward to next year's village fair already.

Wolfgang really outdid himself. I'm definitely starting to like this guy. But that does not mean that I don't like you or that I like you less. I just need you to know that.

PS. I feel like the time has come for you to finally share information with me as well.

Hugs & Love,
Theresa

SIXTEEN

The sun was already shining brightly over the Horse-shoe when Franz got out of his truck in the spacious parking lot. From the main entrance, one could not tell that the building had been erected in the shape of a horseshoe. Carved in between the edges of the white marble construction was a tiny entrance, opening up to a vast park filled with colorful trees and wooden sculptures.

Franz was not your average visitor, though. He had heard about the new town hall Arnold Kraut had recently built way too many times before. He almost felt like he had already been there.

According to Jenny, Kraut's office was located in the geometrical center of the horseshoe, which meant that Franz had to walk through the whole park in order to meet the man he despised so much. It was almost ironic.

Not only had he called his counterpart in Goldau to beg him for a meeting, he now had to walk through the whole perimeter of the construction that had stolen the award for the most innovative town hall in the valley from him.

When he reached his destination, he felt slightly confused. The office of Arnold Kraut was far from how he had imagined it. As he entered through a door in an oversize floor to ceiling window, he found the mayor of Goldau sitting in a Lotus pose with his eyes gently closed. Soft music was playing in the background. In the heartwarming and calming tune, Franz recognized the sound of flutes. The room was out of the ordinary. There was no desk, just a large knee-high wooden table standing on a huge straw carpet. The walls were painted a tawny brown, decorated with the occasional white poster brushed with Asian symbols.

Like in any uncomfortable situation, Franz coughed respectfully to attract a moderate level of attention towards him.

Arnold Kraut took a deep and loud breath.

"Oh man, it is so good to finally meet you," he said calmly without opening his eyes.

Franz didn't quite know how to react.

"Yeah, sure, thanks for taking the time to see me."

"Are you kidding me? Thank you for arranging this!" The mayor of Goldau jumped to his feet and hugged

Franz passionately. "I have been a fan of yours for a long time."

Franz shrugged. "A fan? Of me?"

Arnold nodded euphorically. "Yes, I have heard so many good things from the Commodore!"

Franz smiled. "Oh yeah, the Commodore, he tends to say a lot when the day is long…."

"And I had a dream about you," Arnold interrupted him. "Well, it was more like a vision. I was doing a Kambo cleanse with my shaman a couple of days ago, and I saw the two of us becoming friends."

"Kambo? What's that?"

"They basically put a small dose of poison from a venomous frog in an open wound, and well … it doesn't really matter. What matters is that you are here now. Namaste!"

Franz nodded, although he hadn't understood one word of what Arnold had just said.

"I know so much about you already. I can't believe you are here now. You have been an inspiration for me. I'm sure you don't know much about me, though. The older guys in the party don't care much about the younger ones," Arnold continued.

Although Franz wasn't necessarily proud of it, he knew a lot about the good-looking man in front of him. The first time he had heard his name was back in the city of Graz, during his studies. The Commodore had one day started to talk in honeyed words of a young and brilliant student from Franz's valley. A few years his junior, the young Arnold quickly became a household name in the ranks of the People's Freedom party and amassed a considerable number of supporters in the old ranks as well as die-hard fans within the younger generation.

"Yeah, brah, after finishing my degree summa cum laude in Graz, I packed up my things and moved to Tokyo."

"Tokyo? Wow, that's super far away. How long did you stay there?" Franz asked.

Arnold Kraut placed his palm on Franz's forehead and closed his eyes in meditation.

"I don't really believe in time the way you do. But if I had to put a number on it, I would say around two thousand days." he whispered.

"Why are you touching my forehead?"

"I'm measuring your body energy."

"Oh okay…what's the verdict?"

"Wow, that's remarkable." Arnold said in excitement.

"What is it?"

The young mayor paused.

"You are a panther! A real wild animal, my dear Franz. I haven't felt such strong vibes in a long time."

"A wild animal?" Franz asked, surprised.

Arnold nodded. "Yes, you might not realize it because in your current state, you're like a tiger in a cage."

"What do you mean? Like metaphorically?"

"You're incredibly overweight, and you let people mess with you."

Franz cupped his chin in his hand and thought for a moment.

"So, what am I supposed to do?"

Arnold cautiously slid his palm from Franz's forehead down his body until he reached his genitalia.

"Wow, you have a monster down there. A real snake."

Franz froze.

"I will tell you what I always tell my son: you are a fucker. You should go out there and fuck. You want to be the one doing the fucking." Arnold continued.

"How old is your son?"

"Nine years old, why?"

"And you are telling him to go out there and do the fucking?"

Arnold shook his head. "You don't understand. Doing the fucking has nothing to do with sex."

Franz shrugged. "I'm confused. So, what does it mean?"

"Franz, you have to use your dick energy to fuck people psychologically. Let them know there is a new snake boss in town," Arnold replied.

The mayor of Goldau took both of his hands and placed them on Franz's shoulders.

"Sometimes, the smallest snake in the jungle is the most poisonous one."

"I understand," Franz said.

"Franz Bauer, you are a legend. You need to go out there and show people who you are!"

Franz looked into Arnold's hypnotic blue eyes.

"That is why I am here; I need your help."

Arnold shook Franz' shoulders with power. "Yes! That's what I'm here for. What do you need? Let's sit down at the table and share our thoughts."

"The Commodore called me a couple of weeks ago and told me that he wanted me to build a refugee welcoming center in Maisland," Franz said.

The mayor of Goldau stared at him, puzzled.

"Well, I was wondering if you would be open to also building a small center so we can share the refugees in between our two neighboring villages," Franz continued hesitantly.

Arnold Kraut promptly stood up. "Did you just say refugee welcoming center? Here in Goldau?" The mayor of Goldau ran towards the only shelf in the room and took out two amulets and incense.

"You have to leave now,'" he said calmly while placing the amulets around his neck.

"Leave?" Franz asked.

"No, no, *shamshilahaba*," Arnold murmured while lighting the incense stick with a candle.

Franz jumped up.

"Stop! Don't come closer!" Arnold held his hand up.

"Why, what is happening?"

The young mayor of Goldau was blowing the smoke throughout the room. "I love you like a brother Franz, but I don't need this bad energy in my life right now. You have to leave! It's the best for the both of us."

"What are you talking about?"

"Are you kidding me? A refugee center is the worst karma for any mayor. I feel so sorry for you."

"What about this whole thing about doing the fucking?" Franz continued.

"You my dear Franz, have a dildo up your ass, the size of a baseball bat, don't you feel it? How can you even think about fucking?"

"So, what am I supposed to do?" Franz asked, feeling a bit desperate.

"I don't know, buy yourself a piece of land somewhere far away and leave Maisland for good."

Franz lit up in excitement. "That's it!"

"What do you mean that's it?" Arnold asked, surprised.

"I will buy the land!"

"Okay, great, where will you move to?"

"I'm not going anywhere. I will buy the land where we are supposed to build the center so that there is no more space for such big construction. I am going to call Wolfgang right away and ask him to meet me."

Arnold looked at Franz, clearly confused.

"I will do the fucking Arnold!"

Arnold nodded energetically. "Yes, do that. Go get them. But now, get the fuck out of my office. Thanks. Bye."

SEVENTEEN

The soft yellow light lit up the darkness of the night, moving towards Franz. The mayor of Maisland was sitting on the hood of his truck, hidden by blackness, nervously tapping his hand on his knee. The cigar, anchored between his lips, had died out a long time ago, but he was too caught up in his thoughts to notice.

As the light got closer, it grew in size, cautiously revealing the outline of its source: a forty-year-old Puch Jeep. The military armored vehicle was Wolfgang's most precious belonging. He had put so much love and passion into fixing it that after winning a national restoring competition, a German industrialist offered him a small fortune for it. However, he respectfully declined the offer. Franz waited for him to jump out of the jeep before he slid off the hood of his truck.

"Thanks for meeting me," he said.

Wolfgang looked around. "Sure thing. Interesting spot you picked for this meeting. We're in the middle of nowhere and in the middle of the night. Are you trying to kill me?" Franz forced a smirk. "As much as I would like to, I just don't have the courage to do that."

Wolfgang nodded. "Fair enough. I don't think it's ever easy to kill somebody."

"Well, you should know."

"What?"

"You sell hunting gear, don't you?"

Wolfgang shrugged. "What does one have to do with the other?"

"Let me get this straight. You sell hunting gear, but you have never hunted?"

"I still don't understand the connection you are trying to make."

Franz rolled his eyes. "How can you sell gear that you don't know anything about? If somebody comes into your shop looking for a gun or ammunition, how do you advise them on what to buy?"

"Wait! Are you implying that I don't know anything about the items I am selling in my shop?" Wolfgang asked.

"Clearly, since you just admitted to have never used them."

The man, who reminded Franz of his ninth-grade chemistry teacher, raised his finger in determination. "I have read every single instruction manual, blog entry, and review one can find."

"And that makes you an expert?"

"My dear Franz, I will never be an expert on guns, ammunition, or even fishing gear. But the good news is that I don't have to be. All I have to do is evaluate who the real experts are, collect the relevant information, and pass it on to my customers."

"That sounds a bit half-ass," Franz replied.

"I feel like there is some tension between us. I'll just ask you straight, no beating around the bush, are you mad at me?"

"Of course I'm mad at you, you little weasel!" Franz felt his patience running out.

"Will you tell me why, at least?"

"Wait, let me think," Franz started off sarcastically. "The more guns, less refugees thing, maybe?"

"Oh yeah, we call it the MGLR movement now."

"Whatever, that's not the point. Who cares what it's called!"

"And that made you mad?"

"Of course, it made me mad!"

Wolfgang took a step towards Franz. "I am sorry. I didn't realize it would upset you this much."

Franz shrugged. "It's not like I'm mad. I mean, yes, I am mad, but I do get your point."

"You do?"

"Yes, of course. Do you think I want that stupid welcome center?"

"So why are you planning on building one?"

"Because the party ordered me to build it, don't you get it?"

Wolfgang shook his head. "So why don't you tell them that you just won't do it?"

"Because I can't. That's not how it works, I may be the mayor, but I still have people above me that tell me what to do."

Wolfgang gently tapped Franz's back. "Come, let's sit down and talk about this whole thing."

Franz allowed himself to be led by Wolfgang to the humid grass, where they took a seat.

"To be honest, I myself have been feeling a little overwhelmed by this whole movement thing," Wolfgang confessed.

"I can imagine, it's not easy being in the public eye."

"Exactly, all of these people want something from me now. You know me. I am not an overly social type. I really feel like I've bitten off more than I can chew."

Franz placed an arm around Wolfgang's shoulders. "You are a good guy. And you are by far the smartest person in Maisland."

"I'll try to take that as a compliment."

"You should, my dear Wolfgang. Politics are just not for you. In a perfect world, I wouldn't want that stupid welcome center either, but that's just not how it works."

Wolfgang tilted his head and pressed his lips together. "You are right. I don't know anything about politics and shouldn't get involved in stuff I have no clue about."

"So, will you stop mobilizing people and inciting them against me?"

The nerdy-looking shop owner nodded thoughtfully. "Of course, Franz. It's the only right thing to do. I have other things on my mind right now anyway."

Franz leaned forward. "Oh really, like what? Now I'm curious why you didn't put up more of a fight for your movement."

"That's a very good observation. I am against the welcome center, and I want to do right by the people of the movement, but yeah, priorities change sometimes."

"Come on, don't be so secretive. What is on your mind?"

Wolfgang flashed a crooked front tooth in a contained smile. "Well, if you would really like to know, I have a date tonight."

"Now, who would have thought? Good for you, Wolfgang! I am sure it has been a while since the last one?" Franz said.

The hunting and fishing gear shop owner scratched the back of his head. "Well, I have once visited the salt mine of Bad Aussee with my second cousin Freya, but I don't think that counts as a date."

Franz felt odd sitting in the company of a grown man who had never had a date.

"Better later than never, am I right?" he said, shifting slightly away from Wolfgang.

"I guess so."

"Who is the lucky girl?"

"My date is not with a girl."

Franz's stomach twisted. "Wow, that is quite progressive and obviously totally cool with me. I didn't know you were…I mean, you look so normal."

Wolfgang crossed his arms. "I was what?" he asked in a severe tone.

Franz was desperately trying to avoid eye contact. "Well, I don't know what you guys are called nowadays, but I guess homo-something."

"I am not homosexual! I am forty-seven years old Franz. I don't date girls. I am going to have a nice dinner with a woman in my age group."

Franz breathed a sigh of relief. "Of course you are. I am so sorry, I didn't mean to accuse you of anything," he said, forcing a fake smile. "So, who is this woman? Is she from Maisland?"

Wolfgang nodded. "She is, but a gentleman never tells. Especially because you know her."

"How could I not? Anyway, I completely understand. You are a true gentleman, good for her!

"Thank you. But why exactly did you want to meet me out here?"

"Oh, about that. Nothing. Your movement had put me into a difficult situation, and I needed to find a way out. But after you just agreed to put an end to MGLR, I don't have to go there anymore…"

"I understand. I am sorry that I made your life so complicated the past weeks."

"Don't worry about it. Have fun on your date tonight, my dear Wolfgang!"

EIGHTEEN

Franz's cellphone was ringing. It had been ringing for a while, but he had been sleeping like a bear. After hearing the good news about Wolfgang's intention to shut down the MGLR movement, he had celebrated deep into the night, consuming multiple bottles of apricot schnapps at Jörg's pub. He had run into Günther Frank, the young and utterly motivated new officer of the Maisland police department. In between shots of burning liquor, they talked about the meaning of life and about the love they had for their beautiful Maisland. With each glass, they raised and clinked, a deeper thought seemed to emerge. The pinker their faces flushed, the more they realized that they were not that different after all. They were both introverted people that liked other introverted people. Not necessarily people that were painfully shy, but humans that tended to be more reserved than others.

After the fifth time the phone rang, the vibration pushed the device over the edge of the bed table, slamming loudly onto the wooden floor.

"Bauer," he whispered into the black gadget. His throat felt like sandpaper.

"Finally! It's Jenny," the young secretary said way too loudly into the phone.

"What do you want? It's not even seven in the morning, and I have a massive headache," he grumbled. Actually, it felt more like an ax was planted in his head.

"Did you see what Gabriel Garten posted on Instagram?"

"No, of course not. Why would I? And who the hell is Gabriel Garten anyway?"

Silence.

"Tell me!" he growled.

"It looks like our dear friend Wolfgang is running for mayor."

Confusion sparked in Franz's brain as he desperately tried to connect the dots. "What? How do you know?" he muddled.

"Well, his face is plastered all over Maisland."

Franz's face fell faster than a corpse in cement boots. He jumped up from the bed and dashed out of his house as he pulled on a pair of jeans and a sweater.

Although it was still dark outside, it didn't take him long to spot a huge poster hanging from the church steeple. It was so colossal it covered half of the church. The first thing he saw was a large mustache. Only at a second glance did he put everything in perspective and recognized the happy face of Wolfgang smiling down on Maisland. Under the collar of his white shirt, an olive-green message was addressing the community: 'Wolfgang Mayor, Franz Bauer Traitor.' Almost out of breath, with his heart beating as fast as pneumatic drill and with the danger of running into somebody on the street, Franz rushed back home.

"Oh, good morning!"

A young man with a canary yellow jacket was waiting for him in front of his doorstep.

"It's a bad time now," Franz growled.

"I will be really quick, I promise. I just have one package for you, Mayor. I mean I can still call you that for now, no?" the young man said.

"Of course, you still have to call me Mayor. What else would you call me?" Franz replied, irritated.

"Yes, yes, I am sorry. I just…I mean those posters of Wolfgang all over town are quite something."

"Yeah, that's nothing. It's just a PR gag. Wolfgang is not running, and the movement is dead anyway."

The young postman furrowed his eyebrows. "MGLR is not dead!" he shouted. "As a matter of fact, we have a meeting tonight, and everybody is going to be there."

Franz rolled his eyes. "Sure, we'll see about that."
He grabbed the box and ripped it open.
Inside was a handwritten note and a tiny swing-structure
with five metal balls hanging from fine threads.

Dear Franz,

There is something that you shall never forget:

Freedom and love is what he's looking for
Freed from desire, mind and senses purified
People just want more and more

Namaste,
Arnold Kraut

Franz puffed out lout and grabbed the metal structure.
"What the hell is this supposed to be," he said.
"Oh, I know what that is!" the postman said excited.
"What?"
"A Newton's cradle."
Franz inspected it. "What is the point of it?"
"It demonstrates the principle of momentum."
"Meaning?"
"The principle states that when two objects collide, the
total momentum of the objects before the collision is
equal to the total momentum of the objects after the
collision."

"So, it can't do anything?"

"No."

"OK, get out of here and go do your job," Franz barked.

As he was about to go back into his house, he noticed a white letter sticking out of the pot of his beloved ficus benjamina.

Dear Franz,

How are you?

Yesterday afternoon, I was walking around town, minding my own business as usual, when I suddenly saw a couple of guys walk into our beloved church. They were carrying a very long thin object, and I immediately thought, that must be a large crucifix!

In my mind, this could only mean one thing: we have a new priest (it was about time they found a replacement for that fraud Father Benedikt).

To properly welcome him, I decided to stop by the flower shop to get him some tulips, but then I realized that I didn't have any money on me, so I ended up going back to the church without a welcome gift.

In retrospect, I am glad I didn't have any money on me because as I got there, there was no priest to be found.

As a matter of fact, the church was as empty as a warehouse.

With great disappointment building in my heart, I was about to leave when I heard strange noises coming from the steeple.

Bearing in mind that this is something I usually would never do; I took the initiative and climbed the stairs to the top floor.

As I got closer, the noises increased, and suddenly, I found myself standing next to the men I had seen at the entrance earlier.

In their hands, they were still holding what I thought to be the crucifix. I moved closer to inspect it, but the guys stopped me before I got the chance to touch it. Touch it or not touch it, by then, it was clear to me that the thing was no crucifix. It looked more like a huge rolled-up plastic carpet. Why would they need a plastic carpet in the steeple? Maybe they wanted to get rid of a body? Do you think we'll finally have the chance to witness a murder in Maisland? That would be exciting for once, don't you think so, my dear Franz?

I felt like it was time to leave my comfort zone, and I decided to confront them and ask them who they were and what they were doing in Maisland.

Surprisingly they acted very secretive, and it turned out to be very hard to get anything out of them. Only very reluctantly, they finally told me that they were hired to install an immense poster of the face of Wolfgang, announcing his run for mayor with a sentence along the lines of Wolfgang Mayor, Franz Bauer Idiot.

In my humble opinion: these guys are full of shit. I don't trust one word they said, especially the whole thing about the huge poster. I was there, Franz. There was no poster whatsoever.

Anyways, I ended up taking them to the ice cream parlor afterward, where they consumed a fair amount of ice cream and told me stories about how they usually influence municipal elections all over the country.
Keeping in mind that – as mentioned – these guys are completely harmless, as mayor, I feel like you should be informed about what is happening in our beloved Maisland.

I was inclined to contact Günther Frank over at the police station, but then I decided against it. You know how Günther is, he would have set up roadblocks around Maisland, called forensics, and interrogated the whole town. That is no good for us. When people can't relax and have their minds at ease, they don't eat ice cream.

To conclude: I am getting a little frustrated, my dear Franz. I have the feeling I am feeding you precious information non-stop, and all I get from you is a big pile of nothing. I hope this will soon change.

Theresa

NINETEEN

"He is not in."

"Where is he?"

"It's seven in the morning."

"Where is he?"

"I told you. He is not in."

"What do you mean he's not in? This is a disaster!"

The woman on the other end of the line sighed. "What am I supped to tell you Franz? If he tells me he is not in, he is not in."

"So, tell me where he is!" Franz screamed.

"I told you…?"

"You are the Commodore's secretary. It is your job to know!"

Franz stared at Newton's cradle.

"Do you remember the People's Freedom Party Christmas dinner where we crashed your car into a streetlight?" he said.

"Oh my god. That must have been over ten years ago. You fell asleep on the airbag." the woman replied nostalgically. "Of course, I remember! That was one of the best nights of my life."

Silence on the other end.

"You have a good heart Franz! You know I am not supposed to be sharing details of his calendar, but he is on his way to Maisland."

Rage overcame Franz and he wiped Arnold Kraut's gift off the desk. "I knew it. Motherfucker!"

"Why? What is happening?"

"What is happening is that he fucked me. He is helping Wolfgang."

"Calm down Franz. He is not helping anybody. He was surprised as you were this morning."

"So, what the hell is he doing in Maisland?"

"That I don't know. Maybe he is coming to see you? I would just sit tight and wait for him."

TWENTY

The first rays of the sun had just appeared from east of the valley when five Mercedes S-Class sedans stormed into the center of Maisland with the speed and determination of a Hollywood car chase. Officer Günther Frank had just started his shift when he heard the convoy zooming by the police station way beyond the speed limit.

"What the hell is happening?" he shouted.

An older officer, who had just survived his fifth night shift in a row, gave his young colleague a patronizing pat on the shoulder.

"Let it be Günther, didn't you see the government plates on those cars?" he said.

"What is that supposed to mean? They don't have to follow the rules just because they are politicians?" Günther replied with disgust.

The older officer shook his head. "Let's not start with this again - not today. I just finished a ten-hour shift, I'm out of here."

The young officer was fuming. That's not what he had signed up for.

"I don't care, I'm going after them," Günther Frank shouted while running out of the police station.

As nobody in the station was motivated enough to stop him, the young officer soon found himself in front of Wolfgang's hunting and fishing gear shop. The convoy had taken up all of the parking spots in front of the shop, including the ones for disabled people and electric cars. Günther was so outraged that he immediately wrote parking tickets for all the cars standing on the restricted lots.

"Hey, you, what are you doing?" a tall man shouted.

Günther eyed him up and down. "You parked your car in a restricted area, and I am fining you for that."

The tall man in a black suit approached him. "Do you know whose car this is?" he asked.

The officer shook his head "No, and frankly, I don't care - law is law."

"It's the car of the regional chief of the People's Freedom Party," the man continued with a threatening tone.

Günther smiled sardonically. "Do you know who I am?" he asked.

The man burst out in laughter. "I'm from Goldau, and I read the Maisland Bulletin - of course, I know who you are! You're the one who tried to fine that cow once for walking on a red light."

Günther blushed. "No, that's not how it went down at all. The Bulletin got it completely wrong. I wanted to fine the owner of the cow, but since he was nowhere to be found, I left the fine on the cow."

The man let out an explosive laugh. "How did you even fix the fine on the poor animal?" he asked.

"Everybody keeps on asking me this question. Why do they think that I mistreated the cow? I stuck the piece of paper on its neck with honey." Günther replied.

The guy was almost out of breath from laughter.

"What I'm most known for though, is 'Operation Truffle' – you have probably heard about that," Günther continued.

The man shook his head.

Approximately one year before, the young police officer had successfully spearheaded the most notable and successful operation in the history of the Maisland police department. With the help of two fellow officers, an informant, and a particularly cooperative truffle pig, he managed to uncover a modest mushroom smuggling ring in the woods of Maisland. Following an anonymous tip, the tenacious officer had spent months on surveillance in the area day and night until he caught two Italian nationals *in flagrante*, loading up fifty pounds of chanterelles into the back of their pickup truck. During the interrogation process, it turned out they had been organizing bus tours from Italy to Maisland to steal mushrooms for years.

As soon as the Bulletin picked up the story, the outrage of the population grew exponentially, and after a short but media-intensive trial, the perpetrators received a hefty fine and were declared *personae non gratae* in town by Mayor Franz Bauer.

"I caught a major mushroom smuggling network!" Günther barked.

The tall man stopped laughing. "Now that is impressive. How many pounds of product were you able to confiscate?" he asked.

"Over fifty pounds,"

"Wow that is a substantial amount, well done!"

Günther nodded.

"And what happened to the dealers?"

"What do you mean the dealers?" Günther asked.

"The dealers that smuggled the magic mushrooms, what happened to them? Are they in jail now?" the tall man continued.

"What magic mushrooms?" Günther asked.

"I assume the mushrooms you seized were used as drugs?"

Günther smiled wistfully. "No, they were regular mushrooms. But they were stolen from our woods and in large quantities."

The man burst out in laughter again. "Oh god you are too much to take. This must be the funniest thing I have ever heard. Mushrooms."

"OK that's enough, here is your fine!"

"Thanks officer, I'll make sure to throw it in a trash can and not on the floor. Why don't you do your job and go catch that crazy lady?" he continued.

"What crazy lady?" Günther asked.

The tall man got closer. "When we got here, some weird lady ran out of the shop in her underwear!"

"OK I will look into it. In the meantime, vacate the restricted parking spots. Have I made myself clear?"

"Yes, sir."

TWENTY ONE

Dear Franz,

I don't know why I keep on writing to you.

I should be mad at you.

You never reply to my messages, treat me like garbage when you see me in public and haven't bought ice cream in 453 days – outrageous! If I think about it, the only reason I am still writing to you is that you gave Jenny a job and that you are treating her well as far as she tells me – which is more than anybody has ever done for her. Thank you so much for that.

Anyway, I am writing you to let you know that the suspicions I had about Wolfgang were totally unfounded. I had a longer talk with him and the guy is absolutely innocuous. I wouldn't go as far as to say that he is a nice guy because – let's face it – I don't know anything about him and only met him a couple of times in over two decades.

You should definitely forget about those posters all over town. He has admitted that they were hung up by MGLR members without his knowledge and that he will take care of the costs to remove them as soon as possible. I feel like this whole thing is a huge misunderstanding.

But you don't have to take my word for it. You should pay him a visit yourself and ask him directly. You will get a clearer picture then.

If you feel like it, come over the parlor, we can have some ice cream on me (joking) and talk about it.

Love,
Theresa

TWENTY TWO

For the first time in his life, Wolfgang had fired a handgun. His hands were still shaking as the last smoke clouds egressed from the end of the barrel. As much as he hated the idea of it, it turned out that firing seven magazines of 9 mm bullets into a cardboard deer target had a surprisingly pleasant effect.

After the meeting with the Commodore earlier that day, he had decided that it was time to live a day like a regular Maislander and had turned to the wisdom of Google for help. Although he was looking for concrete suggestions for manly activities, he found himself navigating through a sea of useless blog entries before ultimately coming across a National Gun Association-sponsored article called: 'I fired three hundred rounds a day for the past year and found the man inside of me – what are you waiting for?' The short piece, written by a certain Dr. Jessie Trigger from Alabama, argued that regularly shooting a handgun or rifle is a great way to increase testosterone levels. Dr. Trigger maintained that shooting at least ten magazines of bullets a day could turn any man into an excellent lover. In addition to that, he illustrated a number of indirect positive effects of the hobby, including developing the skillset to professionally shoot a potential robber, molester, trespasser, or the annoying dog of your neighbor.

Being aware of the quality of information available on the World Wide Web, it took Wolfgang a couple of hours to convince himself, but he then eventually decided to go for it. In a surprising state of excitement, he grabbed a box of ammunition and a Glock 17 with the instruction manual from one of the glass shelves in his shop and headed down to the shooting range in the basement.

The exhilaration was so strong and intense that he didn't hear the screams coming from his shop upstairs. Only after his hands stopped shaking and he placed the gun back in its case did he hear the roar of commotion upstairs.

"Where are you?" A man shouted at the top of his lungs. When Wolfgang emerged, he saw Franz, and his face was as red as a ripe tomato.

"Tell me the truth. Now!"

"What are you talking about?" Wolfgang answered, slightly annoyed.

Franz appeared completely out of breath.

"I just heard from Theresa that you had nothing to do with your posters all over town, but I don't believe her. She is a snake," he said, panting as he dropped to all fours. "Did you or did you not partner up with the Commodore to become Mayor?"

Wolfgang shook his head. "The Commodore was here this morning, and he did offer me the opportunity to run as his candidate, but I won't be doing it. And just for your information: he never planned to build a refugee center in Maisland; he just wanted to teach you a lesson. He didn't think anyone would use this as a platform to run against you though."

"How is that possible, are you absolutely sure? Why would he do something like that to me?" A tear ran down Franz's face.

"He mentioned being mad at you for something. And that in his eyes you are a fat pig and that you don't deserve to be Mayor but that he doesn't have anybody else for this and I quote 'in this Godforsaken little village'."

Franz gazed off in the distance.

"But as mentioned, I told him that I don't want to make a deal with him."

"So, you will not be running? What about the movement?" Franz's voice was soft and fragile. "You promised me you would shut down MGLR," he continued.

Wolfgang looked up to the sky for a couple of minutes, immersed in thought.

"Wolfgang? Hello!"

"Oh yes, sorry. Sure, look, right now, I think it would be stupid not to run, especially with the elections only a couple of days away. With the help of all of those damn posters, I am pretty confident I will win in a landslide," he continued in a modulated tone.

"What?" Franz shouted as if he had abruptly woken up from a deep sleep. "You said you would not run, that politics is not for you. What the hell? You fucked me!" he barked.

Wolfgang gifted him what appeared to be a sincere smile.

"Calm down Franz. Let me explain. I will run yes, but once I win, and let me add, by a huge margin, I will drop out for personal reasons, endorsing somebody else as Mayor. The Commodore won't have any other choice than selecting you."

Franz shrugged. "Why don't you just resign now? I'm sure the Commodore will support me then."

"That is very true, but I don't think you will win. You are so unpopular right now. Even if you tell everybody that you won't be building the welcome center, after all, you have lost all credibility. My comrades of MGLR hate you so much they would never vote for you – and they are pretty much the whole male population of Maisland."

Franz nodded. "Yes, yes, I know that. But if there is nobody else to vote for, I will win anyway."

"I wouldn't be so sure about that."

Franz narrowed his eyes. "What? Who?"

"If I was you, I would be dead worried about Madame Theresa. She could easily take it all away from you. She catered ice cream to all the MGLR meetings, and the members love her. Trust me, she has quite the backing from the men of Maisland."

Franz smacked his palm against his forehead. "That sneaky Theresa! You are so right, Wolfgang. Now I understand why she was constantly getting in touch with me. Thankfully I never really fell for her tricks. Especially when she pretended to be all sexy and stuff."

"She is quite the sexy woman," Wolfgang replied, avoiding Franz's gaze.

"If you say so. Anyway, I agree with you. Let's do it your way. I won't campaign and instead will use the time to keep a close eye on Theresa," Franz replied.

"Not too close of a look, though," Wolfgang said, caressing the Glock 17 he had just fired.

Franz tilted his head. "Since when are you such a fan of guns?"

"Don't you think she's gorgeous?" The nerdy shop owner asked.

Silence.

"It's polymer-framed, and short-recoil operated. The world is just such an amazing place."

With a slow and uneasy movement, Franz raised his thumb in what Wolfgang took to understand as agreement.

"Sure, the world is a nice place sometimes," Franz said. "Anyway, can we make sure again that we are on the same page? You will win the election, and then you will resign, leaving the Commodore the decision to put me in power as the candidate that came in second place, correct?"

Wolfgang was still immersed in his daydream. "Correct. This is a great outcome. I am so happy," he replied.

"So am I, thank you so much, my dear friend," Franz crooned. "I am feeling so happy right now. You are doing all of this for me, I really don't know how to repay you."

"Don't worry about it, dear Franz. Just bring positivity into this world, that's how you can repay me."

"Will do! But just out of curiosity, why are you in such a great mood?"

Wolfgang couldn't suppress a giggle. "Well let's just say that my date went pretty well yesterday."

"Oh right, your date." He moved closer to Wolfgang and whispered. "Did you feed the kitty?"

"What?"

"You know what I mean. Did you glaze the donut?"

"I don't understand. You know I don't eat food with too much sugar."

"Come on, don't be shy Wolfy, did you hide the snake in the bush or not?"

"What snake? I hate reptiles."

"Oh my god. Stop being such a gentleman. I want to know if you used your corn dog last night?"

"No, I didn't, we had a delicious Quinoa bowl if you insist on knowing."

Franz rolled his eyes annoyed. "Look, if you want me to spell it out properly, I'll do it. Did you have sex last night?"

Wolfgang blushed. "Ehm, as a matter of fact, I did."

"That's great; how did it feel?"

"Like an explosion," Wolfgang replied, almost over-whelmed by the recollection of the night before. "I am not the same man I was yesterday. I feel so alive!"

Franz clapped his hands. "I am truly happy for you. And very fortunate to call you my friend."

Wolfgang nodded. "We'll do great things together!"

TWENTY THREE

Franz was thumbing through the Maisland Bulletin, a serene and wistful smile on his face. He was in the middle of his morning mantra that he carried out in the comfort of his office toilet.

Defecating to Franz was a premeditated and controlled process. Those precious fifteen minutes after breakfast that he had all to himself set the mood for the day and were of vital importance.

He was going through the last conversations he had with Wolfgang when a sudden bang on the door startled him. "What is it?" he screeched, irritated.

"I am so sorry, Franz. I know I am not to disturb you during your quality time with yourself," his young secretary replied in a tone he found somewhat sarcastic.

"So why the hell are you?"

"A large truck just parked in front of the office," Jenny continued.

"And?"

"I think it's a delivery for you."

Franz exhaled loudly. "What does it say on the truck?"

"Nothing, there's just a logo of an Austrian flag with a weird symbol I don't recognize."

"That's the truck of the People's Freedom Party Jenny, how can you not recognize the logo?" She was such a twit. "OK, I will finish up here and be down in a couple of minutes."

"Ah, that makes sense! Now I understand why the Commodore is here."

"What?" Franz screamed, alarmed. "The Commodore is here? Why didn't you say that right away?"

Franz jumped up and, in less than a minute, was at the entrance lobby of the town hall where he found his old mentor, sitting in a swivel chair.

"Why is this room full of hay? What is this place?" the Commodore said, disgusted.

"That's my hay for the next season."

"And you store it here in the town hall?"

Franz nodded. "I ran out of space at the farm."

"What an idiot. I wish I could make Arnold Kraut mayor of two villages," the Commodore mumbled loud enough for Franz to hear.

"What did you say?"

"Nothing Franzi, nothing."

Franz, crushed, grabbed a chair and sat down next to the Commodore.

"Now that I get to see you face to face, you can finally tell me what this refugee center thing is all about? How could you do this to me?"

"What happened, happened. Let's not cry over spilt milk," the Commodore said. "Let's not waste time on who did what wrong, but let's focus on what we can do now," he continued.

Franz crossed his arms. "I would still like to have an explanation and an apology."

"Fine, I accept your apology. Can we get to work now?"

Franz shook his head in confusion. From the corner of his eye, he spotted the huge van of the People's Freedom Party.

"What's with the truck?"

The Commodore turned around and glanced with pride at the vehicle. "This old beauty here? It is full of promotion material I have brought for you, you ungrateful…"

"Ungrateful what?" Franz replied, hating this man more than he thought possible.

"Nothing Franz, nothing."

"Why would I need promotional material?"

The Commodore looked at him as if struck by lightning. "Are you completely retarded? The election is next week!" he barked.

"I know, but I won't be needing any promotional material."

"Are you kidding me? Have you seen the latest projections? That arrogant, self-entitled Wolfgang has such a lead on you that it's basically mission impossible trying to beat him."

Franz leaned forward. "I wouldn't worry about it if I was you," he said. "I have taken care of everything."

"You have done what?!"

"I have made a deal with Wolfgang," the mayor said.

"Spit it out!"

"He's going to resign right after the election, which means that…"

"I know what that means, thanks," the Commodore said. "But why would he do that?"

"Well, after your visit to his shop, something in him changed. When he realized that the center was never going to be built, he didn't see a need for his involvement anymore. Plus, he really doesn't feel comfortable in the public eye, and he just started dating a woman for the first time in his life."

The Commodore's forehead creased. "That's good and understandable, but why the hell is he still campaigning like there is no tomorrow?"

Franz smiled, as if to say that he had been waiting for that question. "He's doing it for me, to keep up appearances. If he would give up now, somebody else could decide to run at the last second and, considering my approval rate, that would be a disaster."

"And he is doing all of this for you? He seems like a very bright guy, why would he do that?"

"I don't think he's doing it for me. He was serious about the people in his movement and making things right for them. As long as the welcome center is not built, he will be fine with this whole thing."

The Commodore pursed his lips in approval. "I would have never thought that I would ever say something like that to you, but bravo Franzi, good job! I think you are getting the hang of politics after all."

Franz swelled with pride.

"So, are you considering me as your possible successor as the head of the regional People's Freedom Party?" he asked, rubbing his hands together.

The Commodore burst out in laughter. "Not in a million years, my dear Franz."

Franz's face grew hot with shame. "So, I guess you would rather have Arnold Kraut?"

"Oh my god, I love Arnold Kraut. The way he talks, the way he walks…and his suits. They are so tight. They look like a second skin…"

"He is not that great," Franz replied, irritated

"Are you kidding me? Have you seen the Horseshoe? It's an architectural masterpiece. My god, what a man that Arnold Kraut is," the Commodore gushed.

"And he is so hot!" Jenny added from her seat across the room.

Franz closed his eyes in surrender and sunk deeper into his chair.

TWENTY FOUR

Dear Franz,

I'm writing to let you know that I am very disappointed that Wolfgang is not keeping his word. Members of MGLR are still running around town, plastering his face on every surface imaginable. It seems like he is actually running for Mayor, and that is quite the surprise. He fooled both of us.

You know I was always for the refugee center. Not only because it would bring me many more customers, but also because I think that those poor people have a right to come here and to taste Austrian ice cream.

And to achieve that, I would myself run for mayor if that would help. But seeing how strong Wolfgang is with his movement, I don't really see a point in investing time and money for that purpose.

You're a good man Franz, and you have a big heart. Those refugees would have benefitted from a strong and honest man like you. I am sure we will find a way in the future to show our humanitarian side.

In the meantime, stay chill.

Theresa

TWENTY FIVE

Maisland's Alfons Haider high school had been preparing for the election for a couple of weeks already. Bestowed with the great responsibility of hosting all of the town's voting booths, the new principal had taken the opportunity to enhance the infrastructure of the school as a pretext to finally get rid of the life-size bronze statue of principal Schumacher. His predecessor, who was serving a five-year sentence for embezzlement, fraud, money laundering, and heading up a criminal organization, was a very powerful man. Even behind bars he was terrorizing half of Maisland - including the new principal - and according to some, was still running Alfons Haider from the comfort of his cell. Through a straw man, he was passing on information to his network of janitors, cooks, and teachers and keeping a close eye on his successor.

Although the booths had only been open for about two hours, the first tweets coming from the editorial office of the Maisland Bulletin indicated that voter participation was already twice as high as four years ago. Such high participation only solidified last week's polls, which saw Wolfgang with a humongous advantage over Franz Bauer - the only other candidate in the race.

The sentiment among the people was that the mayor was no longer the man that could best represent their interests. And it wasn't so much because of the refugee center affair, which some people had even forgotten about, as it was the missing vitality. What Maislanders had missed most was the energy Franz brought when he was first elected. Four years ago, he had rented a food truck, giving out free sausages in front of the school, the post office, and the police department. He had organized a party at the local lake with free booze and a musical set by the hottest local DJ. He had even handed out vouchers for a free spa day at a two-star hotel in the Slovakian province of Nitra.

This election, however, he hadn't done anything of the sort. The two weeks before the vote, which are considered the crucial days of campaigning and the pinnacle of every candidate's efforts, nobody had even seen Franz Bauer. Rumors suggested the mayor had spent his days in his office, at the farm, and at the lake.

The truth is, the deal he had made with Wolfgang meant that there was no need to keep up appearances and continuing any campaigning efforts.

On the morning when the town would go to vote, Franz wandered into Alfons Haider just as any other regular voter would and approached the booth with the nonchalance of an Imagist poet.

"Franz, it is good to see you! I wasn't expecting you to show up," the new principal said.

Franz gave him a tap on the shoulder. "Why wouldn't I be here? I am still a Maislander, and I have the right and duty to cast my vote."

"Yes, yes I know. But we haven't seen you around in a while. We thought you had waved the white flag already?"

"No, of course not! I am still the best candidate for Maisland. I am the only one that has the political experience, and I'm sure people will realize that."

"Of course, of course…"

"By the way," Franz added in a puzzled tone, "where the hell is Schumacher's statue?"

The principal flickered his eyes in distress. "Yeah, about that. We had to remove it, unfortunately."

Franz stared hard at the principal. "OK…and why is that?"

The man turned scarlet. "It seems we had to remove it to be able to get the booths through the corridors," he answered hesitantly.

The mayor nodded. "That does make sense. I will put in a good word for you with Schumacher before he sends a couple of contract killers to slaughter you."

The principal forced a smile as the color drained from his face. "Thank you so much, my dear Franz!"

"Sure, anything for you. We need to make sure that you remain principal at least until Schumacher comes out of jail. After that, he might as well put you in a brazen bull for all I care."

"What is a brazen bull?" the man asked, his eyes wide.

Franz was enjoying this. "The brazen bull is an old torture and execution device that was designed in ancient Greece. I saw a movie a couple of days ago where they roasted a bad guy in one."

Franz interpreted the silence as a request for more information on the grotesque torture device. "It's an actual bull made out of bronze with a door on one side, in which they install an acoustic apparatus that converts screams into sound. The person – in this case, you - is then locked inside the bull while a fire is set under it, heating the metal until you are roasted to death," Franz continued.

The principal's jaw dropped. "Do you think Schumacher would do this to me?"

Franz's mouth curved into a smile. "Of course not! He is a nice guy; everybody knows that."

Schumacher was, in fact, one of the most feared people in the valley. Rumor had it that he had fed multiple people to his pigs and that he put an enormous price on the head of the young officer Günther Frank for uncovering his wrongdoings.

"I have heard things about my predecessor."

"Nothing to worry about," Franz said.

"I'll take your word for it, my dear Franz," the principal said, trying to appear relaxed.

"So, what happened to your campaign, if I may ask? I haven't seen you around in a while. Have you been busy at the farm?"

Franz nodded. "I was a little absent the last days, I know. I had to direct my energies elsewhere. I can't say too much, but I needed to keep an eye on a possible threat. But in the end, everything turned out to be fine."

He scanned the voting room. "Wait, what is that?" he asked, pointing at a table covered with red baseball caps. The principal blushed. "That table...those are members of MGLR," he replied in a choked tone.

Franz felt his jaw drop. "Are they selling MGLR baseball hats? In here?" he howled.

"Of course not! They're giving them out for free."

"Why would you allow something like that?" Franz asked, but the principal was already walking with determination towards the table.

Franz smiled sardonically. To his surprise, the principal grabbed one of the many red hats and placed it proudly on his head.

"Now you see why I allowed it?" he said with a challenging tone.

Franz clenched his fists. "I cannot believe this!"

The principal moved closer to Franz and whispered. "Do you really think I want you to fill Maisland with a heard of refugees? Can you even imagine what consequences that will have for me?"

"What consequences? Tell me, I'm curious," Franz replied, agitated.

"For starters, I would need to find a way to integrate them in my school. And what about the language and cultural barrier? You think it's easy to organize separate language and religion classes for them?"

Franz laughed. "The refugee center was never going to…" he began before stopping himself.

"Was never going to what?"

Franz quickly bit his lip. He was becoming so careless these days.

"Nothing. Forget about it," he said quickly and disrespectfully caressed the principal's face. "There is an ancient Greek saying, my dear principal."

The principal stepped away from Franz.

"He who laughs last, laughs best," he continued.

The principal gave him a tight smile.

"That's not an ancient Greek saying."

A voice came from behind Franz. He turned around and saw Wolfgang, followed by a legion of MGLR members in red baseball hats.

"The saying has been traced to John Heywood's 1546 book of proverbs. It can be found in the second collection he edited on the subject," Wolfgang continued in his signature lecturing tone.

Franz slumped. He looked in every direction, and all he could see were countless red hats. "Do you mind if we talk in private for a minute?" he said.

"Of course, Mr. Mayor," Wolfgang replied and signaled to his followers to hit the road.

Franz moved closer and grabbed Wolfgang's arm. "I know you have to play your part and everything, but this is a little overwhelming. Don't you think you over-did it a little?"

"I am not following," Wolfgang said innocently.

"Well, how do you think all of these people will react to your announcement after the vote?"

"I wouldn't worry about that," Wolfgang replied.

"I do worry. These people have such aggression towards me, I'm afraid they would rather have me dead than be their mayor."

"I will talk them down. As long as you don't build the welcome center, you will be fine. I promise."

Franz sighed a breath of relief. "So, do you already know when you will be announcing your resignation?"

"I am not sure. Do you have a suggestion?"

"I think you should do it right after the vote count, in your first interview. Once you do that, you can call in a town assembly for the next day where you lay out the details."

Wolfgang nodded quickly. "Sounds good. I will see you later at the Bulletin, I need to go cast my vote now."

TWENTY SIX

The headquarters of the Maisland Bulletin was an iconic two-story wooden house that stood at the periphery of town, surrounded by a grove of maple trees. From the shape of its roof and the generosity of its front porch, it resembled one of the many French colonial houses of New Orleans. While the roof had a signature pyramid-like shape, the porch wrapped itself around the building, creating an external gallery.

The house was built by the owner and founder of Maisland's oldest and only newspaper, Julius 'Diamond' Stein. According to the elders in the city, Diamond had made a fortune in the United States at the beginning of the 20th-century trading gold, silver, and various gems. Ironically enough, he had never traded in diamonds because they only became popular once he had made his way back to Austria as a staggering wealthy man.

With Maisland being his place of birth and Vienna his permanent residence, he spent the remaining days of his life in between his townhouse on Judenplatz in the center of the capital, and his ranch in the countryside, which covered the whole area in between the villages of Maisland and Goldau.

The story of how and why he decided to give birth to the Bulletin is one that, over the years, has been a matter of great speculation and exaggeration. Although most of the elders agreed on the fact that he was just a bored old man in search of a hobby, old relatives of Diamond have stuck with the same ludicrous theory over the past decades.

According to them, at some point in the 1950s, he was given the title of the richest man in Austria, which followed with a first-page article in every influential newspaper of the country. As a result, only a few days later, he had found over fifty direct and indirect relatives in front of his ranch gates, demanding money for the most ludicrous reasons. In a stroke of genius, and because he couldn't find anybody else that would print it, he decided to found his own newspaper and report a fictitious story about him having lost all of his money in a business deal in Rhodesia.

All speculations aside, to this day, nobody really knew why Diamond decided to own such an insignificant media outlet nor why he never intended to do more with his money. After his passing, all he left as his legacy was an uninhabited ranch that "no one else shall ever inhabit" and a local newspaper that banked more money than a Russian oligarch.

As a tradition in Maisland municipal ballots, on the night of the elections, the political actors, the chiefs of police and fire, other pillars of the community, as well as regional journalists, were invited to the Bulletin's headquarters to watch the projections.

Mayor Franz Bauer was in a particularly good mood that night. He appeared at the doorstep of the Bulletin in his Sunday attire, and a large smile spread across his face. His positivity was so radiant that a very uncomfortable Berthold tried to calm his excitement by laying out the newest polls.

"Hi Franz! Good to see you. You seem very happy. Have you heard anything about the latest polls?" the reporter asked.

Franz smiled. "I have not! You know I'm not a numbers guy."

"Well," Berthold said in an uncomfortable tone. "I'm afraid Wolfgang has over 98% of the votes," he continued.

Franz shrugged. "Again, I'm not a numbers guy. What does that concretely mean?"

Berthold struck a thinking pose. "Let me see. According to the latest polls, you should have around a hundred people voting for you."

Franz looked bewildered.

"Your extended family includes more than a hundred people, which means that not even your whole family voted for you," Berthold said, eyeing Franz for a reaction.

"Well then, I guess it shall not happen," Franz replied.

Berthold's face turned from highly uncomfortable to slightly suspicious.

"OK if that's the case, then you don't have anything to lose anyway," he said and watched Mayor Bauer walk away.

In the meantime, the main room of the colonial house had filled up with guests. The large reception table was covered with lobster canapés and French champagne, courtesy of the Maisland Bulletin fund. Old man Diamond had meticulously set up contracts to ensure that the Bulletin would always exist as an independent entity. He had calculated that with the capital he had left in the fund and taking into consideration inflation and developments in the consumer index, the Bulletin would be able to survive at least until the year 2625. To prevent embezzlement and overspending, he had capped spending on every possible and imaginable expenditure, be it employees, marketing, or even office supplies, except for the municipal election night.

As a result, since his passing, this one specific event had turned into the embodiment of a spending spree. Over the years, it had happened multiple times that the Bulletin had spent a couple of years' budget on catering for

174

one single night. During the last election, which Franz Bauer had won in a landslide, Berthold had even booked David Hasselhoff for a private performance, which likely abbreviated the existence of the Bulletin for a couple of years.

Out of all the guests present at the event, this year's guest of honor – Wolfgang – stuck out like a fly on a wedding cake. He was definitely not enjoying himself as much as he should have been. From the moment he set foot into the wooden construction, he had been approached by people nonstop. Some of them had even addressed him as Mr. Mayor already. While shaking such a large number of hands made him sick to his stomach, what surprisingly irritated him more than anything else, were all of those people congratulating him for his harsh stance towards the welcoming center as well as towards migration.

"Are you ready for your big night?" an overexcited Berthold shouted.

"What big night?" Wolfgang asked.

Berthold's nose crinkled. "Well tonight, obviously. You know the election and so on."

Wolfgang forced a smile. "Sure, yes, my big night, I am excited!" he replied, devoid of emotions.

"What can we expect from our next mayor?" Berthold continued.

"You will have to ask him," he answered.

"What do you mean? You will be the next mayor!" Berthold said, befuddled.

"Oh yeah, correct. Sorry, this is all so new to me. I haven't really given it too much thought, to be honest."

"Come on Wolfgang, you are one of the smartest people in Maisland. I am sure you can give me something."

"Well, thank you, I will try and take that as a compliment. I'm afraid I really don't have anything for you."

"But it's for your beloved Bulletin, please!" Berthold said in a rather desperate tone.

Wolfgang's eyebrows waggled. "Fine! The only thing that I can tell you is that Maisland is up for a big surprise."

Berthold's face lit up in excitement. "I will make sure to spread the word, Mayor!"

"Thank you. In the meantime, I would like to ask you a question." Wolfgang said.

"Anything, Mayor!"

Wolfgang looked around. "Who organized this event?"

Berthold's face lit up with pride. "I did!"

"I have been calculating the costs for all of this in my head: the champagne, the canapés, and even the lobster – including the recent spike in prices of up to 48% due to the ongoing strike of container ships from east Africa – and I wondered why you would spend so much money for such a useless event?"

Berthold froze.

"I mean, you could have bought a set of twelve Steyr Aug rifles for all of that money," he continued.

"Well, it is a tradition here at the Bulletin. Long before I took the helm and began organizing the event." Berthold said.

"I understand. I am just not sure if Mr. Stein would have appreciated it," he said as he glazed over at a portrait of old man Diamond.

"Well yeah, but he is not among us anymore. Anyway, the results should be in at any minute, lets gather everybody," Berthold replied as he cleared his voice with a loud cough.

"Ladies and gentlemen," the reporter screamed at the top of his lungs. "Please all gather in the living room; the results should be in very soon."

As everybody rushed into the main room of the house, Berthold was tuning into the regional news channel. The young presenter was sitting on a table, holding a pile of white papers in her hand.

"And now, let's look into the first results of the election for mayor in Maisland," she said. The room went quiet. As everybody held their breath, she continued. "As you see in the infographic behind me, newcomer Wolfgang of the movement More Guns, Less Refugees is projected to score 99%."

The Bulletin's headquarters exploded in applause. Every single person in the room moved towards the incumbent mayor to congratulate him on his massive victory.

"And now let's go live to Maisland where we have the chief political editor of the Bulletin on the line with the new mayor," she said.

A very embarrassed Berthold quickly ran towards the mayor with his phone on video call mode.

"Thank you for having us on your program," he shouted into the phone.

Half of the television screen was now occupied by Berthold's arm, lifted up in selfie mode and the embarrassed face of Wolfgang.

"Congratulations on your victory, Mayor! How does it feel to win?" the news anchor asked.

Wolfgang lifted an eyebrow. "Frankly, it makes me lose all hope in humanity."

"Great, congratulations again!" the anchor continued as if she had not heard him. "What will the first items on your agenda be now that you are in charge of the great town of Maisland?"

"I have no idea. I haven't really thought about it." Wolfgang replied.

"That's great! I am sure Maislanders are already excited about your impressive ideas," she said.

"We received an anonymous tip just before the program saying that you would have a big announcement to make?" she continued.

Wolfgang shook his head. "No announcement, sorry."

"Great! But wait, who is that lovely blonde lady next to you? Is that the new first lady of Maisland?" the anchor asked. Wolfgang smiled. "As a matter of fact, yes, she is. May I introduce my partner Madame Theresa."

Theresa smiled into the phone camera. "I happen to own the best ice cream parlor in the valley. You should all come!"

"Wonderful. Best of luck from us, and thanks for talking to the channel."

Surrounded by well-wishers, Wolfgang glanced sideways towards Franz.

The former mayor was white as chalk. His eyes and mouth were frozen wide open in an expression of stunned surprise.

TWENTY SEVEN

"You did it," she said while clinking her champagne glass with his.

"I couldn't have done it without you," he replied quietly.

"You were already leading the polls before our first date…"

He smiled. "Should I let in some more hot water?"

To celebrate the landslide win and to release themselves of the stress of the past weeks, Wolfgang and Madame Theresa had decided to treat themselves to a romantic bath.

Wolfgang grabbed Theresa's leg and started rubbing her foot. "I really couldn't have done it without you. I mean not properly, at least. You make me a better person."

Madame Theresa smiled dreamily. "Oh, come on Wolfy. How am I making you a better person?"

"The whole refugee matter. You opened my eyes."

"I'm happy you see it my way now too."

"Of course, it's the only way to see it, those poor people. How can we not offer them help?"

"That's what I have been saying from the beginning. How can we look away?"

Wolfgang nodded.

"Have you been thinking about what we discussed a couple of days ago?" she continued while caressing the inside of Wolfgang's leg with her foot.

The newly elected mayor blushed. "Ehm, of course, I have,"

"So?"

"It's not easy. I expect a lot of backlash. To be honest, I don't think it's possible in my humble opinion."

Madame Theresa moved her foot up, reaching his genital area.

Wolfgang's eyebrows waggled. "I mean, I agree with you," he stuttered. "It is the right thing to do."

"So do the right thing and build the welcome center Mr. Mayor," she said in a theatrical tone.

Wolfgang chewed on his lower lip. "Even if we overcome all the backlash, the city has no money to build something like that. Franz Bauer spent all of the village's money for those stupid eating contests."

Madame Theresa scrunched up her face.

"I wouldn't even have a problem giving the village my large plot of land next to the sports center for free, but that still won't solve the liquidity problem," he continued.

Theresa's eyes sparkled.

"I think I might have a solution for us," she said.

"What?"

"How about we make a public-private partnership?"

"What are you thinking about?"

"You know how I have been working really hard all these past years."

The newly elected mayor nodded.

"I have saved up quite the amount of money," she continued. "I could finance the whole construction."

Wolfgang looked at her with suspicion.

"And what would you like in return?"

"Very easy, my love. I want to have the ground floor at my disposal, that's it."

"And what do you want to do with it?"

"I'm thinking about setting up a huge ice cream parlor that can be used by the refugees as a canteen."

Wolfgang puffed out loud. "I don't know if a public/private partnership is the right thing to do as one of my first initiatives as mayor."

"Of course it is, my love."

"And how would that work with the building? I mean, if you pay for it, how can the city use it as a refugee center?"

"I will lease the village the whole building except for the ground floor for…let's say twenty years?"

Wolfgang shook his head. "I sincerely doubt that we can afford the lease. Once the refugees are here, we will eventually get money from the government, but before that, I can't commit to anything this expensive."

Theresa splashed her hands in the water. "We can't wait that long! If word gets out, there will be such a backlash that we won't be able to proceed," she said. "Look, how about I just lease the building to Maisland for free, and we'll divert some government money once the refugees get there? I trust you to do it right by me once this thing is through. But we need to start right away," she continued.

Wolfgang tilted his head. "I guess we could make it work like that. But I'm still not sure that we'll be able to pull it off."

"Think about all of those poor refugee children, dying of hunger," Madame Theresa said.

"I know, I know. But I still have a bad conscience about how we deceived Franz Bauer. He is a good man, and we fooled him."

"Bauer is a moron; forget about him."

"Don't say that; he was always very nice and respectful to me."

Madame Theresa leaned forward and grabbed Wolfgang's penis.

"If you don't want to do it for the refugees, do it for me, my dear Wolfy," she whispered and winked awkwardly.

Maisland's new mayor bit his lip and stared up to the ceiling.

"Fine, let's do it," he surrendered.

Theresa jumped up in victory, splashing water everywhere.

"Great, I already talked to the construction company; they could start in a couple of days."

"That was fast."

"There's no time to waste when it comes to saving lives!"

"I guess so."

Madame Theresa dried her arms with a towel and grabbed an envelope from the bathroom cabinet.

"I also drafted a welcome letter in your name for the refugees. We should let them have it as soon as they arrive in Maisland," she said while passing the paper to Wolfgang.

Wolfgang hesitantly took the envelope.

"Sure, my love, anything for you."

"Thanks, baby. Make sure to call the interior ministry in Vienna right away to inform them about your decision to build the center."

Dear friends from afar,

Welcome to the great Maisland!

As the mayor of our beautiful village, it is my duty and great pleasure to greet all of you.

Life in our little alpine community is exciting and diverse. We are surrounded by mesmerizing mountains that provide a playground for countless outdoor activities, as well as breath-taking views.

Most of your fellow Maislanders were born here and have never left our valley, so the environment is perfect for an exchange of views and cultures.

Although in my function as the first citizen I am strongly encouraging all Maislanders to welcome you with unlimited sympathy and the utmost respect, let me also take this opportunity to give you a quick and gentle warning: not everybody here is thrilled about your arrival. An unforeseeable number of citizens started a movement called More Guns, Less Refugees. Although the name of the movement might sound innocuous, I can confidently say that its members are very dangerous. Don't ask me why they hate you, because I have no idea. I imagine it has something to do with the preservation of Austrian culture. I don't understand it, and as far as I know, most people in Maisland don't either.

One part of our culture on which we strongly pride ourselves is our culinary diversity. Our dishes are delicious and full of nutrients. I won't bore you with a list of the various recipes – there is really no need. To remain practical, I will just mention one example: ice cream.

I don't know if you are familiar with this culinary masterpiece, but it represents without a doubt a milestone of Austrian cuisine. *
Here in Maisland, people consume ice cream for breakfast, lunch, and dinner. **

And guess what? You are in luck! Coincidentally, a brand-new ice cream parlor just opened up under your new home, featuring a grand variety of five different flavors, including vanilla, chocolate, strudel, Mozart ball, and (for the adventurous ones) coconut.

Also, please don't forget that you can/should/must exchange your government food stamps for ice cream vouchers from the parlor. I can only emphasize that it is a great, clean, and delicious parlor.

If you have ice cream-related questions, feel free to contact the first lady at any time. Here are her details:
theresa@besticecreammaisland.at

For all other questions and complaints, feel free to get in touch with:
questionsandcomplaintsmaisland@gmail.com

See you soon,
Mayor Wolfgang

*I cannot guarantee the accuracy of the Information
** I really can't

TWENTY EIGHT

"Did he call back?"

"No, he didn't."

"Did she call back?"

"You know she doesn't have a phone."

"What about the hunting and fishing gear shop? Did you go there?"

Jenny nodded. "Yes, it's closed for vacation."

Franz blinked slowly. "What about the ice cream parlor? Have you been there?"

"Closed for renovations."

"You got to be kidding me." Franz banged his hand on the desk. "This can't really be happening," he muttered.

"Why do you need to speak to them so urgently?" she asked.

Franz looked at Jenny with a mix of astonishment and rage. "Are you kidding me? Have you been following anything that has been happening in this fucking village lately?" he barked.

Jenny shook her head. "Not really, you know I don't care much about politics."

Franz grabbed a stapler. He was dangerously close to throwing it at her dumb blond head. Instead, he took a deep breath. "You need to find your mom. Where the hell is she? Has she vanished from planet earth?" he asked cynically.

"I don't think that she actually vanished from the earth. That only happens in movies. I don't know what else to say, she hasn't been home in a couple of days," she pursed her lips as if thinking. "She must be with her new dumbass boyfriend."

"Who? Wolfgang?"

"Yeah. Oh my god, that dude is so uncool."

Franz swallowed his retort, trying to keep a cool face.

"Just out of interest, how long have they been dating?" He asked softly, trying to sound composed.

Jenny lifted an eyebrow. "It hasn't been that long, maybe a couple of weeks?"

Franz sighed out loud. Every time his young secretary opened her mouth, he got angrier. "You do understand that it's not only important for me that we find Wolfgang or your mom, but also for you?" he said, accompanied by a fake smile.

Jenny shrugged. "Important how?"

Franz clenched his teeth so vigorously that he could feel them grinding down. "How unbelievably stupid," he said, before biting his lip. He looked at Jenny again. In her eyes, he saw nothing but confusion and worry. "Look it's quite easy. If I am no longer mayor, you no longer have a job. Do you understand now?"

Jenny's brows snapped together. "That's not what has been told to me," she replied in a challenging tone.

Franz's face twisted. "What? What have you been told?"

"That once Wolfgang is moving in here, I'll get a promotion."

The mayor's face dropped. "Who told you that?" he barked.

"My mom!"

Franz completely froze. Anger, pain, shock, and frustration were swirling inside of him.

"When did you talk to her?" he asked, his voice choked from rage.

"Just before. She came by the office a couple of hours ago," she replied cheerfully.

Franz gazed into the distance. He felt the blood completely drain from his face. Every part of him was on pause while his thoughts were desperately trying to catch up.

"Are you feeling ok?" Jenny asked.

Franz's whole body was trembling as if he were sitting on a washing machine.

"You don't look good Franz, maybe you should go see a doctor," she said in a gentle but scolding tone. "Oh yeah, and I almost forgot, my mom, left a letter for you," she continued, holding an envelope in mid-air. Franz looked up at his secretary. His eyes were bloodshot and glassy as he grabbed the piece of paper.

Dear Franz,

It has come to my attention that you have been desperately looking for ways to contact the new mayor and myself.

I imagine that you wanted to congratulate Wolfgang on his win and on our fresh love story - that's so sweet of you. Many thanks from both of us.
We're in cloud nine since we came into each other's lives. Sometimes what you want, and need is right in front of your face.

We would also like to take this letter as an opportunity to congratulate you on your campaign. You have fought bravely, and you have been a gracious opponent. Who would have thought that it would have ended up being such a close call between the two of you?

Nonetheless, as the fair man you are, I'm sure you realize it's in your best interest to have a smooth handover of all functions to Wolfgang. We should have a meeting about this soon.

I'll be on his plot of land next to the sports center over the next couple of days. Feel free to come by if you have time - which I imagine you do since you're not mayor anymore ;)

Ciao,
Theresa

TWENTY NINE

The speedometer needle was shaking vigorously, pushing 180km/hr. The anomaly on the dashboard, however, did not impress Franz. On the contrary, he took it
as an invitation to put even more pressure on the gas
pedal of his beloved ten-year-old pickup truck.

Dashing towards Wolfgang's building plot next to the
sports center, he was thinking about all the possible op-
tions on how the conversation with Madame Theresa
would play out. He had quickly dismissed the initial idea
of punching her in the face before even saying one word
- that would not have been constructive, and besides,
Wolfgang might shoot him. Thoughts wandered
through his mind related to the countless letters he had
received from Madame Theresa and to all the live en-
counters they had had in the past months. Franz was so
caught up in his thoughts that he didn't even notice the

many empty trucks passing by in the opposing traffic lane.

The former mayor would have easily stayed buried in his thoughts for longer if it wasn't for a strange yellow figure in the distance that was getting bigger and bigger by the second.

He took a hand off the steering wheel to rub his eyes.

The mysterious yellow figure had revealed itself to be a massive Liebherr crane. The first thing Franz associated with the impressive machine was a YouTube video he had seen some time ago, where a man broke a Guinness world record by jumping from the top of a similar crane into a swimming pool with only 40 cm of water to break the fall.

At second glance, he also noticed a great movement of heavy road vehicles coming in and out of the sports center, so he quickly dismissed a world record event as a possible explanation for what he was seeing.

As he got closer, he also started to notice the outline of a huge building surrounded by hundreds of workers.

Befuddled and full of questions, he parked his truck and walked towards the building, spotting a construction worker with long blond hair.

"Theresa?" he barked.

She was standing next to a cement mixer wearing an oversized orange construction helmet, with a sizeable construction map in her hands. She turned around and waved at Franz.

Although construction had only started that day, the progress the dozens of workers had achieved in the first hours of the morning was remarkable. Not only were they able to finish pouring cement into the outline of the base, but they had also already started erecting the outside walls.

"I take it you received my letter," she said while walking towards the former mayor.

Franz felt confused. He had a million questions even before reaching the building plot, and now he felt like he had a million more.

"What in earth's name are you building here?" he asked. Theresa turned around and pointed at the construction site. "This little thing? I'm just expanding my business and building a new ice cream parlor!"

Franz pursed his lips. "This place looks way too big for an ice cream parlor."

"No, not at all. I mean, maybe I will make a restaurant out of it," she replied nervously.

"A restaurant? There are already two restaurants in Maisland, and they have barely enough clientele to survive. I don't know how you will fill this huge building." Madame Theresa winked at Franz.

"Anyway, I don't really care about your stupid new parlor. That's not why I am here," he continued.

Theresa nodded. "Oh yes, sure. You want to talk about the handover of your duties. I understand. Unfortunately, it's a bit of a bad time. I need to be here at the construction site for the next couple of hours."

Franz's eyebrows snapped together. "What? Are you kidding me?"

"What do you mean?" she looked at him with big, innocent eyes.

"You guys fucked me. I had a deal with Wolfgang, and he betrayed me."

"Oh, okay, that's why you are here. I don't know anything about that."

The former mayor smiled sarcastically. "Don't play dumb with me, Theresa. You think I didn't notice how flirty you were with me when I announced my intention to build the refugee center? And what about your letter, telling me that Wolfgang is innocuous and that I should not worry? You trapped me."

"No Franz, that's not what happened." Theresa gently grabbed his arm. "Come on, let's go sit under the big tree there."

"Let go of my arm," he said roughly, shaking her off.

"Look, Franz, I'm going to be very honest with you. I'm going to tell you everything," she said.

Franz crossed his arms. "I'm waiting."

"It is true. I have flirted with you. But not only because I wanted to have the refugee center built for my own financial gain but also because I like you. Since you never reacted to my advances, I stopped. And then I met Wolfgang."

Silence.

"And sorry, but what did I get from this whole thing anyway? It's not like the refugee center is being built. I would have preferred for you to remain mayor, but then I found love, and that was more important to me than financial gain. You have to believe me!"

"You still fooled me, convincing me to trust Wolfgang," Franz barked.

"I didn't! At the time, I didn't know Wolfgang actually wanted to become mayor. He only changed his mind after that and asked me to not tell you. What would you have done in my position? I love him."

Franz closed his eyes in frustration.

"It is just so unfair," he said, his voice choked. "I really believed him when he told me that he supported me and that we had a deal."

"I know. I'm sure he feels bad too. But his strong morals and the urge to do right to the movement and to Maisland ultimately prevailed."

"I still want to talk to him," Franz said quickly and with determination.

Madame Theresa shook her head. "I don't think that's a good idea," she replied.

"Look, Theresa, I don't care if you think that it's a good idea or not. He can't hide from this forever. I will find him."

"This thing is over; let it go Franz!"

Franz took a step towards her, his face contorted into a menacing look. "This is far from over - I can promise you that!"

THIRTY

"Get in!"

Franz turned around.

At first, he only saw his reflection in a shiny, black mirror. He took a step back and realized he was looking at a car. His eyes wandered towards the passenger door, where the window was fully down.

"Come on, it's me!" the voice screamed again.

Franz pushed his head through the window and saw the gorgeous face of Arnold Kraut.

"How did you creep up on me like that? I didn't even hear you," Franz replied.

The mayor of Goldau smiled pretentiously. "It's a Tesla, Franz. You should get one too if you care about the environment."

"Everybody keeps on telling me about the environment. Is it some new trend?" Franz asked.

Arnold Kraut pushed the passenger door open. "Just get in. We have to take care of something."

Franz obeyed and squeezed himself into the trendy electric car.

"It's a little tight in here. I don't know if it's the right car for me," Franz said, huffing.

"Don't worry about it; you can't afford it anyway."

"Alright, thanks. So why are you here?"

"I just wanted to show you my new car Franz. And to remind you that you can't afford one."

Arnold Kraut punched the former mayor on the shoulder. "I am kidding Franz!" he laughed. "I mean, I am not kidding about the car, I'm pretty sure you can't afford it, but that's not why I am here," he continued.

"So why are you here then?"

Arnold hit the steering wheel with his palm. "The refugee center. We have to stop it!"

"What refugee center?"

"The one Wolfgang is building next to the sports center. Wait, you don't know about it?"

Franz felt faint. "What? How do you know that?" he stuttered.

"Jenny told me, that's why I assumed you'd know too."

Franz shook his head left and right, utterly confused, trying to put the pieces of the puzzle together.

"Wait, how do you even know Jenny?"

The mayor of Goldau smiled brightly. "Oh, I have sex with her. Around three and a half times a week," he replied.

Franz shook his head in disbelief. He was unsure what to ask next. "What does three and half times mean?" he said, confused and paused. "Actually, forget it. What should we do about the refugee center?"

"I already talked to the Commodore about it. Unfortunately, there is nothing that he can do. He called Vienna and asked them to stop the process, but they laughed in his face. They told him, and I quote: 'If a mayor is dumb enough to call us with the intention to build a refugee welcome center in his town, we cannot reward his stupidity by not taking the offer.' The only person that can call off this whole thing is Wolfgang himself, and he will, sure as hell, not do that. We're on our own..." Arnold Kraut replied.

Franz nodded. "I appreciate you being here. But why are you helping me?" he asked feebly.

"Are you kidding me? I can't risk the refugees integrating themselves. That could open the door for another center, possibly in Goldau. Plus, the inhabitants of Goldau were not amused when they initially heard about your plans to build the center. I mean, I'm the mayor of a town neighboring this shithole."

Franz scratched his head. "That makes sense, fair enough. So, what is the plan?"

Arnold Kraut seemed giddy with excitement. "We're driving to the police department, and we're going to convince them to stop the works."

"Alright! Let's see how fast this fancy car of yours can go."

Franz smacked his hand on the bell for the third time. Frustration was building up inside of him. His savior, Arnold Kraut, had just broken seven traffic rules to get him to the police department in a matter of minutes, and now that they were finally here, not a single police officer was in sight.

"I can't believe nobody is here," he said, befuddled.

The mayor of Goldau placed his palms on Franz's cheeks. "Patience, my dear Franz. Patience."

Franz was about to jump over the counter when a voice appeared from an open door in the back of the room. "Yes, I am here. Coming right out."

A couple of seconds later, the young Günter Frank rushed towards them as if his boxer shorts were on fire. His uniform was impeccably ironed, and his hair combed into a center-part.

"I am so sorry. I was just in the back going through the cold cases of the past two centuries," he said, a little out of breath.

Franz's eyes lit up. "Wow, that sounds mysterious. How many cold cases do you have there Günther?"

"I have not been through all the documents yet, but so far none," he replied, seeming disappointed.

"Oh great, that sounds very interesting. Anyway, we need to talk to the chief," Franz announced.

"I'm afraid he's not here."

Arnold Kraut signaled to Franz that he was going to take care of the situation now and pushed him aside. He looked deep into the young police officer's eyes and flashed his very white teeth.

"You know who I am right?"

Günther Frank nodded energetically, holding a hand in front of his right eye.

"I'll ask you again, would you please call your boss?"

Günther Frank raised his second hand and placed it in front of his other eye. "Your teeth. You're blinding me. Would you please close your mouth?" he said, annoyed.

Franz slammed his fist on the counter. "We don't have time for this Günther. Where the hell is everybody else?" he screamed.

Günther looked shocked. He had rarely seen Franz Bauer so agitated. "The mayor," he stuttered before interrupting himself. He looked at Franz a little embarrassed. "I mean, the new mayor, Wolfgang, he invited the whole department on a fishing trip."

Franz puffed out. "That slimy Wolfgang. So why the hell are you here then? Nothing happens in this village anyway," he said, annoyed.

"I won't be bought! You know how I feel about gifts and stuff like that," he said firmly.

"Yeah, yeah I know, you are a really good boy Günther," Franz replied.

Arnold Kraut's expression hardened. "OK fine. That means that we need you to do something for us now."

"Sure, how can I help?"

"You need to stop the construction work down at the sports center," Franz jumped in.

"What? I can't do that."

Franz grabbed the officer's arm. "You don't understand. Madame Theresa is not building an ice cream parlor. She is building a refugee center," the former mayor said with imploring eyes.

Günther Frank laughed out loud. "That is ridiculous," he giggled. "I know she is building something together with Wolfgang, but I am sure that it's not a refugee center," he continued.

"How can you be so sure?" Arnold Kraut asked.

"Because it's Wolfgang. For Christ's sake, he was the one that started the MGLR movement. He was voted in exactly because he was against the welcome center, hello!"

"Listen to us!" Franz shouted, with his palms pressed on his forehead. "There has to be something somewhere."

"I looked into the whole thing, Franz. You know me. As soon as I noticed the first construction trucks driving through Maisland."

"And?"

"It's all by the books."

"How is that possible?"

"The building is a public-private partnership."

"Meaning?"

"Meaning that Wolfgang, representing Maisland and Madame Theresa made a partnership."

Franz nervously tapped his fingers on the counter. "I'm getting confused here, Günther. Please explain the whole thing to me from scratch."

"Sure. So, Wolfgang as a private citizen leased his plot of land to the village for free for twenty years," he said in a lecturing tone.

Franz nodded.

"Madame Theresa, on the other hand, agreed to pay for the construction of the building and to lease the whole building, except for the ground floor, to the village for twenty years for free," he continued.

Arnold Kraut jumped up. "There you go. Why do you think she would do something like that? Leasing it out for free…there must be something else in the contract," he barked nervously.

"There was nothing else. Yesterday, I told Theresa to show me the paperwork, or I would slow down construction until everything is sorted out, and what I saw is what I told you."

"We need to know more about the partnership. Wolfgang and Theresa should clear everything up. What the hell do you think the village will do with the building? It will become a refugee center!" Franz shouted.

"I agree. But I can't do this without asking the chief. I'm so close to getting fired. I can't even afford to lose a department pen. I'm going to talk to him as soon as he is back, I promise."

Arnold Kraut laughed sarcastically. "As if that will do anything. The chief is out on a fishing trip with Wolfgang, do you really think that he will confront his new best friend?"

The young police officer shrugged. "That's all I can do for now guys, I am sorry."

THIRTY ONE

Dear Franz,

My sources told me that you went to the police station with that pretty boy Arnold Kraut earlier today.

I really don't understand this move from your side. If you have questions regarding what I am building on the plot next to the sports center, why don't you come directly to me?

Since we have known each other for a long time and respect each other, I will do you the favor of clarifying the whole thing with this letter. I hope you appreciate my kindness.

Regarding the building, I am erecting it's absolutely none of your business. I suggest you stay the hell out of it, or you will feel the consequences. Are we clear about this, you fat pig? If I find out you talked to any-body about this, I will personally make sure that you'll never be able to speak a word again in your life.

You are done! Just get over it and get on with your sad little life.

With zero love,
Theresa

THIRTY TWO

"How did it go?" she asked, caressing his back,

"Good. I talked to the chief. He is going to let us alone for a while," he replied in a worried tone.

"That's good news. We can't have them sniff around. Especially with the free lease for Maisland," she replied. "I mean, they can't legally force us to talk anyway."

"It's a small village, Theresa. Nobody forces anybody to do anything. The chief has a lot of people asking him about the construction, and he just wants to make sure that everything is fine," Wolfgang replied.

"Yes, of course, I understand. But he said he would leave us alone, right?"

"I know. But he wasn't happy about it. Günther Frank has also been putting a lot of pressure on him."

Wolfgang looked up to the ceiling.

"But he agreed to let us alone, right?"

Wolfgang nodded slowly.

"So why are you worried?"

The mayor leaned forward, escaping her grip on his shoulders. "I'm not sure I can go on with this much longer. I feel like I am lying to everybody around me."

Madame Theresa pulled him toward her and kissed his forehead. "I know. You have to stay strong just a little longer. In a week's time, the construction will be almost ready, and then you can tell everybody," she replied.

Wolfgang shook his head. "I'm not sure we can wait that long. Franz Bauer is walking around telling everybody about the refugee center."

Theresa clenched her fist. "That motherfucker, I'm going to take a knife and…"

Wolfgang looked at her, alarmed. "And what?" he asked.

"Nothing, nothing, Wolfy. He just makes me very angry," she said, gnashing her teeth.

"So, what do you suggest we do?" she continued.

"I think I should give a statement to the Bulletin. An invite to the *Festhalle*, where I will address all Maislanders," he said with a decisive tone. "What do you think?"

"Yeah, that's not a bad idea. That will win us a couple of days for construction," she replied. "I will draft something for you right away," she continued.

"No, not this time Theresa," he replied firmly.

Her eyes bored into him.

"It needs to be me writing it. You're going to have to leave it to me this time. Plus, I have already done it," he continued, drawing a note from the pocket of his jeans.

Dear Maislanders,

I want to take this opportunity to thank all of you for your support – especially my comrades of More Guns, Less Refugees.
You came out in record numbers to vote for change.
Change is what I promised, and as much as I would like to follow up on my promise, the undeniable truth is that populist ideology has poisoned the healthiest of organisms in our society.
The truth is that – as 21st century Europeans - we are obliged to follow up on our duty to preserve and enhance moral authority. History, which undoubtedly repeats itself, has shown us that marginalization and discrimination has only led the path to authoritarianism.
To address these issues and reverse the path of destruction we have been flirting with for too long, I would like to invite you all to the Festhalle tomorrow at 8 p.m.

For safety reasons, I would recommend you leave your weapons at home.

Yours,
Wolfgang

"I don't get it," Madame Theresa announced.

"It's ok. I don't think anybody will."

She shrugged. "Then what's the point?"

"The point is to not reveal anything," Wolfgang replied. His counterpart looked lost.

"The key is to write a lot of meaningful words, in no apparent order and without really saying anything," he continued. "A simple invite would incite too much speculation. People would start assuming things, and we don't want that."

"I am starting to understand," Theresa said.

"As long as people are busy trying to understand what I am trying to say, they won't start guessing what I could possibly announce and so on."

Madame Theresa nodded. "Alright, my love, this time we're doing it your way."

THIRTY THREE

Wolfgang had clearly underestimated his fellow Mais-landers. Since his announcement was printed in the Bulletin, the mysterious invite to the *Festhalle* had been the talk of the town. Some villagers speculated that it might have something to do with Franz Bauer. The former mayor had spent the past days walking around Maisland like a preacher and warning everybody of an imminent wave of migrants and the collapse of Maisland's infrastructure.

While a couple of elders found themselves genuinely worried about Franz, most of the proud inhabitants of the rural village found it ironic that the former mayor had lost his mind and was now the one warning them against something he had been pushing all along.

The curiosity around the announcement ultimately overtook the confusion, and all of Maisland decided to show up for the big event at the *Festhalle.* As a precaution, Wolfgang had hung a large sign in flashing colors next to the entrance of the outdated building: Members of MGLR, please leave your weapons in your trucks (included are hand grenades, rocket launchers, butterfly & throwing knives, as well as scythes and chain saws).

While the heavily intoxicated crowd was already singing traditional Austrian songs, the newly elected mayor was sitting backstage, waiting for his big moment. The chants were so loud that he almost had to hold his hands on his ears, which fueled his nervousness even more.

"It's time to go out there," Madame Theresa said, grabbing his hand.

Wolfgang nodded. The time for his big announcement had finally come. He took a deep breath and walked into the main hall. The crowd exploded in cheers. Members of More Guns, Less Refugees were waiving cardboard guns in the air, and women danced in their traditional dirndl dresses.

"Wow, thank you all for coming out tonight," the new mayor said into the microphone. "Especially to all of my dear comrades of the MGLR movement. We have achieved quite something together."

The crowd celebrated him with a standing ovation. "Wolfgang is the best; forget about the rest," MGLR members chanted.

Wolfgang blushed.

"Thanks, guys!" he shouted, waving his hand to the villagers. "I don't want to waste too much of your time tonight, so I'll get right to the point. I had announced that I would give a statement, and that is exactly what I'm going to do," he continued.

In the first row, which as usual was reserved for important Maisland figures, Franz Bauer was rooted in his chair, nervously tapping his fingers on his lap. He couldn't take his eyes off Wolfgang. He had so much aggression towards him that he had to fight back the urge to run up on stage and tear into him like a wild beast. But he refrained. In a couple of seconds, Wolfgang would himself tell everybody the truth and - ideally - be lynched by the same crowd that was cheering for him right now. Franz smiled sardonically.

"But before that, I need to make a public apology to Mayor Franz Bauer," Wolfgang said.

He waited for every eye to turn to the former mayor before continuing. "You are a great man, and you know why I'm apologizing. I hope that soon we'll be able to be friends again."

Franz rolled his eyes.

"I called you all here because I wanted to talk to you about something very important," Wolfgang continued. "What I have seen in the past weeks, ever since I started the MGLR movement, is division - and I hate it," he said. He paused.

The room full of villagers fell silent.

Wolfgang looked around the crowd, trying to make eye contact with as many people as he could. "We cannot live like this. There is a vital need for compassion among us. What kind of 21st century citizens would we be without it?"

He paused again. Murmurs began to erupt in the crowd. "And it starts right here. MGLR members versus other citizens, Maislanders versus Goldauers. This has to stop," he continued in the same serious tone.

A young MGLR member raised his hand. "Hello Wolfgang, congratulations on your win again; we are unbelievably proud of you," he said, slightly uneasy.

The mayor gave him a thankful smile.

"But what exactly are you trying to tell us?" the young man continued.

Wolfgang nodded complacently and pointed at Theresa. "With the help of my dear partner, I decided to build something to remind all of us of what it means to be there for each other and to live in harmony with our neighbors and friends," he said in a gentle tone and grabbed Madame Theresa's hand.

Murmurs grew louder. He glanced sideways towards his new love, who in turn gifted him an encouraging smile. Wolfgang grabbed the microphone and bent it towards him. "Friends, friends, quiet down. There is nothing to worry about," he said cheerfully.

As the crowd started to hush, Franz Bauer jumped from his chair. He had had enough of this cheaply acted drama. He turned around and faced the crowd.

"Why don't you get to the point and tell everybody here that you have built a refugee center," he screamed at the top of his lungs.

The room turned so silent that you could have heard a needle drop. Wherever Franz looked, he saw wide eyes and open mouths.

Wolfgang's forehead creased. "What are you talking about, Franz?" he said in a calm tone. His mouth curved into a smile.

The former mayor turned around and stared straight into his eyes. "Come on, Wolfgang, the jig is up. You can no longer take these poor people for fools. Tell them what you are building next to the sports center!" he shouted in a challenging tone.

Wolfgang gazed back at him with an ingenious grin and nodded. "Alright, Franz. I wouldn't have wanted to do it this way, but you are right; the people have a right to know."

Franz smiled sarcastically.

Wolfgang cleared his voice and moved closer to the microphone. "I want to start by apologizing to all of you here. I have not been very transparent with you since I got voted into office," he started off.

"Just be a man and tell them!" Franz shouted. He was losing every single gram of patience he had left in his body.

Wolfgang grabbed the podium with both hands. "Fine! As I said before, I wouldn't have wanted to tell you all this way, but as my first project as mayor, I built Maisland a modern and state of the art community center!" he shouted, his gaze wandering straight into Franz Bauer's crazy and confused eyes.

It took the former mayor a couple of seconds to process the information, but right when the rest of the *Festhalle* exploded in joy, he felt a hole in his stomach the size of a crater. He glanced towards Theresa, who was standing next to Wolfgang, and saw the shock register on her face before she could hide it. His intense gaze in Madame Theresa's direction couldn't have been translated into anything other than a request for an extensive explanation.

"We will have a digital library, computers, a free gymnasium with a spa area, a climbing wall, and lots of rooms for arts and crafts as well as language and yoga classes and other activities…" he continued.

Theresa turned and promptly kicked Wolfgang in his calf. "What the hell are you talking about," she whispered loud enough for the first row to hear.

Wolfgang ignored her and continued distributing thumb ups to the crowd.

As the noise slowly dried out, a woman in the second row waved towards Wolfgang to get his attention. "But I didn't think we had any money left for such a big project?" she screeched.

"Thank you so much for your question, my dear," Wolfgang said and pulled Madame Theresa next to him on stage.

"Fortunately, my beloved partner was generous enough to build the new community center for us and to lease it to the town for twenty years for free."

Madame Theresa's face turned scarlet. She looked ready to explode. You could almost see the flames swirling in her eyes. She grabbed Wolfgang's arm and stuck four fingernails into his skin.

The mayor swallowed the pain and put up his most genuine smile. "Ladies and gentlemen, please give it up for Madame Theresa," he said into the microphone, clapping his hands and trying to shake off the talons.

The villagers unanimously rose to their feet and gifted Theresa with a similar standing ovation to the one they had given Wolfgang only moments earlier. Among the many clapping hands were those of Franz Bauer. Wolfgang watched him, unsure what to make of his predecessor's reaction. There was no indication that his smile was forced. Actually, it seemed pretty apparent that it came from deep inside of him, lighting his eyes and spreading into his whole body.

"Well played," Franz silently mouthed when his laughing eyes met the humble gaze of his successor.

THIRTY FOUR

Dear Theresa,

I am sorry I only came back to you now. It has been quite busy the past couple of months, as I am sure you have noticed.

Let me take this letter as an opportunity to apologize to you. I have not been giving you enough attention in the past months, and I am fully aware of it.

Since Wolfgang became mayor, my life has become much more relaxed. I can spend time on the ranch, taking care of the animals and of myself. Apart from not having to deal with all the bureaucracy of being in office, the best part about my newly found freedom is that

I don't have to pretend anymore. I can tell people what I think to their faces with no repercussion - so good!

I take it that you must be devastated after what happened at the Festhalle. I can't even start to understand what is going on inside of you. Besides your - I imagine by now failed - relationship, you must have lost so much of your beloved money building the new center for us. Hereby let me just say that we are all extremely thankful for that. You were absolutely right that night I announced the refugee center. It was about time for a new building.

There is really nothing you wouldn't do for Maisland. I heard from Wolfgang that you agreed to rent out the ground floor of the building to the village too, and for such little money - so generous of you. I imagine that it wasn't easy to run your brand-new, huge parlor with a couple of guests a day. The decision to rent it out is a win-win situation for all, I think. I am sure that the laser tag facility will print even more smiles on people's faces than your ice cream.

Regarding your wonderful daughter, Jenny. I tried to convince Wolfgang to keep her as his secretary, but he told me, and I quote: 'I think that a one-eyed goat with the memory of a goldfish would do a better job than her.' I mean, you can tell that he has great respect for her, but it's just not a good fit somehow.

In the hope of making your life a little easier, I took the liberty of telling Günther Frank to have a proper look at your books and at the expiry date of the ice cream you are selling.

P.S. Your ice cream tastes like crap.

Love,
Franz

ACKNOWLEDGMENTS

Writing a novel is harder than I thought and more rewarding than I could have ever imagined.

My biggest thank you goes to Freya Hübner. By now, you have probably read the novel more often than I did. Nobody is more obsessed with finding a missing dot, and that speaks for your commitment.

I am also very grateful to Kirsten Donaghey for the great editorial work she did on the novel and for taking the time to meet me during a pandemic.

Thank you to my family. To Roberto, Gerlinde, Greta and Nikita.

ICE CREAM FOR REFUGEES

Printed in Great Britain
by Amazon